A PHOENIX RISES

Jemma Ward's dream of a happy family home with her fiancé, Luke, is shattered by his obsession to chase a dream of riches. Her self-esteem plummets further when, in a restaurant in Kuala Lumpur, Jemma must dine alone because Luke has stood her up. Resolving to break free and take control of her future, destiny intervenes when Adam Li saves her from an attacker. At her lowest point, there's only one way for her to go — and that's up!

VALERIE HOLMES

A PHOENIX RISES

Complete and Unabridged

LINFORD
Leicester

First published in Great Britain in 2010

First Linford Edition
published 2010

British Library CIP Data

Holmes, Valerie.
   A phoenix rises.- -(Linford romance library)
   1. Love stories.
   2. Large type books.
   I. Title II. Series
   823.9′2–dc22

ISBN 978–1–44480–489–8

Published by
F. A. Thorpe (Publishing)
Anstey, Leicestershire

Set by Words & Graphics Ltd.
Anstey, Leicestershire
Printed and bound in Great Britain by
T. J. International Ltd., Padstow, Cornwall

This book is printed on acid-free paper

1

Jemma replaced her chopsticks on the plastic rest at the side of the small plate next to her rice bowl. The perpetual noise from the radio, the irregular rotation of the overhead fan and the overpowering humid heat had a draining effect upon her as she waited, surrounded by the constant chatter in a variety of languages from the other diners. The effect was of a constant hum, and then Jemma tuned in to the English voice resounding from the radio, which spoke out over all other Chinese dialects, offering words of wisdom and advice between songs and snippets of news or topical events. She listened to the DJ. 'If you see a blind person crossing the road, slow down, because you never know, they may not see you coming!' The voice's latest tip struck a humorous note with Jemma; she loved irony.

She stared at her watch. Luke was late. He should have been here by now. To be stood up was bad enough, but to be stood up in a road side restaurant in the heart of Kuala Lumpur was too much, like the heat. It was he who had suggested the place, yet it was her who had arrived and eaten alone.

Sometimes she wondered if he even realised just how distant from him she felt. How was she going to tell him that she wanted a separation? He never listened to her. Hints certainly did not penetrate his determination to achieve his latest plan. He just expected her to fall in with it, whatever it was — like sitting in a roadside restaurant in a foreign land — waiting for him to arrive. The only reason she had agreed to his latest rendezvous was so that they could part amicably, or at least appear to; bitterness was not an emotion she liked to cling to. She hoped he would see it that way. She had never broken off a relationship before. In fact, she had never had a proper relationship like theirs before but, that only made the pain deeper. The commitment appeared to run one way only.

Luke was a man of priorities and rapidly she had found to her horror that she appeared to be further down on his list than the monetary ones. So instead of a meal between two friends, she had eaten alone, surrounded by strangers talking in a mixture of unusual tongues; mainly Cantonese or Mandarin dialects.

Discreet, dark, curious eyes stared at the solitary western woman who had sat silently eating and drinking at the corner table. Luke would have to have a good explanation this time.

The rotation of a fan overhead provided a welcome breeze, which wafted across her, carrying the smells of spicy, hot food on what was yet another very humid day. You could never go hungry in this country. The food was ample and varied; tantalisingly exotic and cheap. Fruit was plentiful and larger and fresher than any versions she had seen in the supermarkets at home.

It was a land of colour, variety and choice. Despite the humidity she found it fascinating in its simplicity of life, complexity of culture.

Sipping her ice cold Milo, she left the money on the small plastic plate with a tip. She supposed her loneliness also played a part in her disappointment because everywhere around her were groups of friends or families enjoying each other's mutual love of the food on offer. It was the first time she had acknowledged how alone she was feeling since arriving at Kuala Lumpur International Airport.

'Nihao!' One man stood up and greeted another, shaking hands animatedly, obviously friends judging by the warmth they showed.

'Hi,' his friend replied.

Jemma saw the two sit down. Food was ordered and drinks served. Friend talked enthusiastically with friend and Jemma's loneliness grew. Her patience spent, she had to leave.

Jemma had chosen nasi ayam, a

simple but delicious dish of chicken rice. She waited for the lady to take her ringgit and stood up, noting the radio was now playing a different sort of music in the local tongue, one celebrating 'Merderka — Malaysia', 50 years of independence, and why, she thought, shouldn't they? After all it was their country and people deserved to rule themselves. Applying the same logic and resolve to her own life, she was determined that she would take control of hers and not let Luke dictate to her any more. What had Emily Pankhurst suffered for if a modern woman was still under the rule of a man? Luke was such a dominant character, so full of energy, vision and determination — his own, though. If she suggested something that differed or threatened his viewpoint he would deride it and she would back away rather than confront him. It was strange, she reflected, how the very qualities she had initially loved him for were those that she now loathed in him. He hadn't changed at all, but she had; she had grown and learned, and the sensitive Jemma, which he said he loved, was slowly being killed off, replaced by a more worldly cynic that would laugh mockingly at another country's well-meaning safety bulletins echoing from their radios.

She left. Luke had had his last chance to talk to her, to show her that he would listen and that there would be a mutual love to hang on to, and he had blown it. She was annoyed that her common sense had not suggested that they had met within the safety of the hotel, but he had insisted that nowhere made Laksa like this small restaurant did; it was renowned as the best. By whom he had not said, but he would still try it out.

Crossing the roads here was not an easy task for anyone, but she had become braver about holding up her hand and stepping out into the constant flow of traffic. This was a very different world to the cold, blustery, north-east town back in England that she had grown up in. Anybody, whether able or disabled was brave to venture into the road where a myriad of vehicles seemed to have the right of way, and yet somehow there was an unspoken code between the pedestrian and drivers that allowed for a relatively safe passage.

Jemma made her way carefully along the uneven paving slabs that lined the street. This was an old street or 'jalan', traditional and ramshackle in style, vastly contrasting with the new shopping malls where anything you wanted could be bought in opulent surroundings. They would challenge any found in the west. Here, all the stalls and restaurants were plying for business, promising the casual onlookers the very best of noodles, satay and other local Chinese, Indian or Malay dishes such as 'roti canai'. The smells and colour, like the noises filled the air, puzzling her senses as she walked along deep in her own thoughts. The uneven pavements and open roadside drains added an element of danger to her adventure.

This was an exciting and different world; as a newcomer she read the brightly coloured shop signs, written in different languages. They were glaring yet attractive in a cheerful bright way. Luke, she thought, should be here, sharing this moment with her enjoying the unique experience, holding her hand and explaining what these foods were, and how life here works. Then, as if a sixth sense was working unknowingly in her subconscious, a further thought crept in — he should be protecting her. Where was he?

She looked at every new sight and listened, yet she felt as though she were set apart from it in her own bubble. The heat had drained her energy and the disappointment her heart.

Jemma was too deep in her thoughts to even notice the car approaching at her side.

'You want teksi, miss? I show you around the city.'

Jemma realised that the voice was speaking to her as she looked down and saw a man leaning out of a slightly battered taxi cab.

'No . . . No, thank you,' she answered politely, walking on around a haphazardly parked motorbike.

'I very cheap, miss. Take you see the Petronas Towers; best and highest in the world,' the man insisted.

'No, really, I've already been there . . . thank you,' she replied, increasing her speed, anxious to turn down the alley opposite her hotel and away from the persistent man.

The taxi man muttered something in a language she did not understand and drove on. Jemma was so relieved that she slung her rucksack onto one shoulder and continued on her way. She hadn't even noticed the motorbike's noisy engine as it approached from behind her because she was concentrating on walking safely toward the cut-through to the alley opposite her hotel which represented a safe haven away from the city's noise and constant bustle. The first she realised that she was in danger was when she felt a strong jerk on the bag's strap. Instinctively, she clung to it and was almost dragged off her feet. Fearing she would be run over by a car if she did not relinquish it, Jemma let it go despite the panic she felt inside her. Her passport and most of her money were in the hotel room's safe, but it was her liberty and freedom that she saw disappearing with her bag. Jemma was vulnerable and alone in a strange land of different cultures, without support . . . Without Luke!

2

Jemma watched the drama unfold as the man in flip-flops, tee shirt and jeans rode off without glancing back at his prey, only to be taken by surprise himself, when a Chinese man punched him in the side as he was going to make his escape. The bike went into a skid as the driver lost control along with his balance. The 'have a go' hero's reactions were quick as he ran a few feet to where the thief had hit the ground and retrieved her bag by yanking it off him. The biker was equally as swift. Springing to his feet, he jumped astride his motorbike swearing, she supposed, profusely at the bystanders who backed off, and then he sped away through the gap between the gathered onlookers.

Jemma was shaken and embarrassed by all the attention she was getting, yet grateful to the stranger who stood before her holding her rucksack. He was quite tall; perhaps five foot eleven as opposed to Luke's six feet two inches. Without asking, he placed a hand on her shoulder, nodding politely to the strangers as he spoke in different tongues to the people around them. The people dispersed and he helped her up. He swung her bag onto his own back whilst determinedly walking her in the direction of her hotel.

'Thank you,' Jemma stuttered because she was shaking; she couldn't seem to stop. Pliantly she followed the stranger's guidance. They left the commotion behind them, to Jemma's relief. Gradually she regained control of her body. The comparative silence of the alleyway made her suddenly aware of being in a narrow snicket between two restaurants with this total stranger who still carried her bag. 'Where are you taking me?' she asked, more than a little nervously.

'To your hotel, where you can have a calming drink and gather your wits.

Where you will be safe. Are you hurt?' he answered her in a clear English voice with little trace of an accent.

He let her walk slightly ahead of him as they manoeuvred past some piled up cardboard boxes at one side of the end building.

'You speak English,' she replied, and instantly regretted stating the obvious, but her nerves were shaken and she had never felt so vulnerable and alone since Luke had told her they should sell up and discover their own space again. That simple phrase had resounded like a death knell to their relationship. Luke had said more but there was no need; she had realised the love between them was not equal and was mainly one way. He wasn't ready for settling down or marriage; he had tried to 'tactfully' tell Jemma this. She had been totally taken aback because they had a home. Why had they bought their lovely house if not to make their nest in preparation for their own future? He had even made sure it was in a good location for the

13

local sought after school. So she had been certain of what he wanted from their relationship, as she did — a family house, a family home, a future. But Luke was quick to point out once they had moved in that they would make quite a profit if and when they sold up, before the predicted recession hit, and they would be free to start over again wherever they liked, after a good holiday, when house prices dropped away. During the few days Jemma had been in this fascinating yet bustling city waiting for him to arrive from the Hong Kong office, she had joined a trip to Penang Island. Once a quiet resort, now traffic and condominiums had arrived and with them the peace she had remembered there had gone. It had taught her one valuable lesson: you can never return to what had been, and she wished she had not taken this journey, but it had been a necessary visit. It was the place she had first holidayed with Luke, her about-to-be-ex fiancé. He was the reason why she was here, a token gesture, a holiday as friends, before they went on to their next venture; only she didn't want to go on — not with him. He would go back to the UK, and Jemma, she was contemplating travelling further to visit Australia. That was where she would stay for another month at least, but she had not told Luke this yet, as it was no longer any of his concern.

In so doing he had made Jemma feel as though she was the added bonus to the investment plan and it had hurt her deeply, destroying her ideal romance, her home and their future.

So far this 'holiday' was not turning out to be her idea of a good time either. Now she had a sore knee, her hand still shook and she was in a narrow alley with a total stranger after becoming a victim in the main street.

'Yes, miss, I speak English,' he answered politely with the hint of a smile on his lips, but she guessed was too polite to openly show his amusement at her naivety, or was it stereotypical ignorance. His eyes did, though, deep and dark, yet they had a sparkle to them of an impish humour.

'What about the police?' she asked. 'Surely I must file a report or something, mustn't I? I could have been badly hurt.' There she was asking for guidance again from a man, and this time from a stranger.

'Was anything stolen, miss?' He gave her back her bag and folded his arms casually.

'No, I don't think so. He had no time to even look inside thanks to your quick thinking.' Jemma knew he was aware of this but he was making her see the situation as it was.

'Are you hurt or injured, miss?' he replied, without any great concern showing, as she was obviously not injured and he had handed her bag back to her in one piece.

Jemma shrugged dejectedly. 'No, you retrieved it safely, and except for my pride, I am also unharmed. However, I was attacked, you saw it and so did all of those people.' She pointed back towards the main street that thronged with strangers.

'Did you see his face? Could you describe his bike?'

'It was red and rust,' she said and Jemma saw him shrug.

'So are many of them. Have you any witnesses?' He looked at her impassively.

Jemma was starting to feel more than embarrassed; she was reluctantly annoyed with her rescuer's manner. 'No to the first few questions, but yes to the last. You, for one, are a witness.' She folded her arms also.

He guided her by her elbow as they crossed the busy road in front of the hotel and looked at her as they passed by the hotel's doorman. 'Let me buy you a drink inside. We can talk much better in there, in comfort.'

'Who are you? How do you know where I am staying?' She clung to her bag and stared at him, hoping he did not notice she was still shaking slightly.

'Because, miss, I am staying here also, I was behind you when you checked in, and besides, you need a drink, I think.' He smiled and glanced at her trembling fingers, then gestured with his hand that they continue inside.

The thought of being in the cool, dry, air conditioning away from the heat, humid air and perpetual traffic noise outside decided her to turn and walk into the hotel foyer. The stranger followed and led her to a fairly secluded corner of the lounge. He ordered tea for two and then sat down opposite her. For the first time he looked slightly less confident than he had out in the street.

'Have I thanked you yet?' she asked, not really remembering if she had or not.

He nodded.

'I should reward you,' she said awkwardly.

'Then you can pay for the tea if you wish.' He smiled and she sensed he was teasing her.

'No point in filing a report then,' she

admitted, and instantly he agreed.

'Bag snatchers are quite common, miss. They are cowards who prey on easy targets — like you; females that are on their own or by the wayside. Were you lost or just taking a short cut from the shopping mall to the hotel? In future it would safer to use the walkway up there. He pointed through the window to some steep steps which led to the metro, where the LRT joined sections of the city. Did you intend to see the city on your own, miss?'

'No, well, yes, I suppose so. I have been looking around on my own but I am meeting my fi . . . friend here. He was delayed, though — business.' She rummaged inside her bag to make sure that all was safe and well, knowing it could not be otherwise but glad to create a distraction for a few moments.

The tea arrived and was set out on the table for them. He poured it out and handed her a cup.

'You were very quick . . . and brave. Who are you?' she asked after sipping the comforting drink.

'I am Adam Li.'

'You are not Chinese then?' Jemma shook her head thinking she must have lost her senses. What on earth was she saying? 'I mean you're not . . . '

'It is OK. I know what you mean. I have a Chinese name too but I chose Adam myself, when I was studying in the UK.'

Jemma smiled. 'I'm so sorry, you must think me so ignorant.' She drank her tea, her hand still shaking slightly.

'No, I think you are in shock and understandably so. Give yourself a few moments to recover. I am not so easily offended by a few simple questions. Let me show you around the city tomorrow.' He was watching her, calmly waiting for her reply.

'I don't know what to say. I don't want to intrude on your holiday and besides . . . ' Jemma placed her cup back on the table then looked around as if Luke should be there, expecting him to have turned up, wondering if a message awaited her in her room, 'my friend may yet arrive, or leave a message for me. I am uncertain of my plans until he does.'

She thought she saw a slight shadow of disappointment cross his face when she said 'he' then dismissed the thought as a fanciful notion.

He continued, 'I'll take you to your room if you are anxious, miss. If your friend does not turn up I would be able to meet you for breakfast at nine, if you are still feeling a little shaken and would like company after your ordeal. There is a safe way to see the sights, if you know a 'local boy'.' He grinned broadly and she could not help but see how there was a youthful, fun loving side to this confident young man.

'You are a very determined, 'local boy', aren't you?' she said as they stood up.

'I would like you to feel safe again and for that you might need a little help and a friend,' He stepped back so that she could walk around in front of him.

21

'Thank you, Mr Li. You are very kind, but I can see myself to my own room.' She did not mean to sound prissy or ungrateful but the world was starting to move at a faster and stranger pace. She needed a night's sleep and calm her nerves before contemplating what she should do tomorrow. Right now, today had been enough to cope with. Tomorrow the idea of hiding in the beauty salon of the hotel suddenly held great appeal.

He nodded respectfully and stood back a little more. She walked to the lift without glancing back, and entered it. When the doors closed she felt safe and cosseted.

Once she saw her own room door, emotions swiftly washed over her. She was safe, but felt shaken all over again and a little tearful. She desperately wanted to snuggle into the bed, aircon on, and dream it all away. Jemma felt alone again, but she would wake up stronger and know what to do tomorrow. She swiped her door key card in the lock, and saw the little light turn from red to green. The lift pinged and the doors opened. Mr Li stepped out.

She looked at him, surprised, then sternly, but he just nodded at her, a slight smile playing on his lips as he walked to the room two doors away from her own and swiped his own card in the lock, grinning back at her, and entered his room.

She smiled to herself. He had been behind her when she checked in; of course he could have a room so near her own. Jemma had not even noticed him. She entered her own room, locked the door firmly behind her, placed the key card into the slot which instantly triggered her aircon and lights into action. With her conspiracy theories over, the kindly Mr Li had been an absolute gentleman and had a room two doors away from hers. He had so bravely brought down the robber, who could have been armed for all he knew. She would have to reward him.

Malaysia was a country of three main

races — Malays, Chinese and Indian — and their unique cultures. The style of life was so varied; modernisation was face to face with the way of a simple life, contrasting and occasionally clashing with the desire to be seen as a truly modern and upcoming country.

Like all places there were things about it she loved — like the dragon fruit, mangosteens, papaya and lychees to name but a few of the glorious exotic fruits she passed on the market stalls. The longan fruit grew on woody stalks a little like grapes; once its outer shell was peeled the inner sweet, almost translucent, fruit was revealed — gorgeous. Then there were things she disliked, like the larger rough shaped fruit of the durian, the odour from which lingered and caused it to be banned from public places like lifts. Like the motorbike bag snatchers, it left a bitter taste in her mouth, similar to the relationship with Luke.

3

The next morning she showered and felt refreshed. A good night's sleep could cure a multitude of problems except for one — Luke. No text message, no message from the hotel concierge, no phone call. She dressed and decided she would go for breakfast. It was 8.30 a.m. Jemma remembered the events of the previous evening and if it had not been for a light bruising on her knee and a slight rip on the outer pocket of her rucksack she may have decided she had just had a nightmare. If it had been, she had dreamed of an unlikely hero, a mysterious man who had stepped from the crowd and defeated her attacker. Jemma decided she would meet him at breakfast as he had offered. She had sent a text to Luke and he had not answered. She picked up her room key and left her phone in her room.

The restaurant had an impressive display of buffet tables laid out with a colourful selection of breakfast choices to please all tastes and cultures. To Jemma they looked lovely, certainly offering more temptation to the taste buds than a bowl of cereal back home. Everything was freshly made and presented in an artistic and pleasing way for the eye to admire. The hotel was one of the best in KL and, unlike some of the more run down ones she had stayed in, this one was managed with the utmost efficiency, cleanliness and thought for customer care and satisfaction.

Jemma saw a young couple seated together, gazing happily into each other's eyes as she entered the restaurant. She was standing at the buffet picking out slices of freshly chilled water melon and papaya, when she glanced across to the table slightly behind the gold and cream pillar next to the dim sum server; she adored the pork steam buns known as 'Char Sui Pao'.

Seated at a table to the side of the pillar was her rescuer of the previous evening, Adam Li. She looked at him and smiled. Jemma had recognised Adam instantly; his friendly face was watching the entrance. He was there sipping his coffee until he saw her, then he quickly replaced his cup and gestured for her to join him.

The waiters and waitresses wore embroidered gold edged jackets that complemented the light decor of the restaurant. They smiled at everyone, serving coffee and tea to the people as they were seated at their tables. Efficiently they cleared away dishes as if unseen, overseeing the smooth running of the place and seeing to the needs of the guests who came and went at will.

The loving couple were completely absorbed with each other; they paid little attention to their food and surroundings let alone anyone else in the restaurant. Sadly, she reflected how quickly a romance can fall apart, a dream so real and solid one day, like her and Luke, so real that you could almost touch and embrace the love, yet it could be so easily shattered the next, like her own had been. Yet she was determined to regain her self esteem and find the old Jemma; make a fresh start using the money from her half of the sale of their beautiful home in Tunbridge Wells, Kent. It all seemed like another life a world away.

Adam seemed pleased that she had acknowledged him. It felt strange that she should want to talk to this stranger at breakfast, but she did, mainly to thank him properly for his quick thinking and bravery the evening before. Also, she wanted him to see her looking calm and composed in his presence, unlike the jabbering wreck who had quivered pathetically before him the previous evening. She didn't know why it should matter to her what image he carried of her within his head, but it did.

During her fitful sleep the whole scenario had taken on an ethereal quality, as if she had dreamed the whole set of events. She had mulled over how weak she must have appeared as she had trembled visibly at the shock of the attack before him. It had felt like an after tremor to the main shock of actually being targeted by the bag snatcher. Was that how shock affected people, she wondered? Post traumatic stress, she remembered reading once.

'Mr Li, I hoped to see you this morning and thank you properly for helping me. I was a little shaken yesterday and . . . I must have looked quite foolish and . . . '

A waiter appeared slightly to her side and pulled out a chair at the table so that she could join Mr Li.

'I . . . ' She had paused long enough to collect a small plate upon which was balanced a fork with a piece of dragonfruit and sliced papaya.

'You must join me, please.' He took the plate from her and placed it on the table opposite his. 'Please, sit down and do not worry yourself about thanking me again, for you already have.' He spoke to the waiter in what she recognised as Mandarin and instantly a place was set for her, before the man discreetly left them alone.

'You seem to be a person who is both very persuasive and authoritative, Mr Li.' That grin appeared across his face, impish yet quite charming. His dark brown eyes almost glistened with the humour they held behind them. Jemma wondered if she genuinely made him smile or if he was laughing at her in some fashion; either way he was pleasant, polite and his manner radiated warmth, unlike Luke's which had always hid a cynical edge. She was puzzled why she should be comparing Mr Li to her ex, but it was something she had already done quite a few times. The shock of the attack must have affected her in some way, she reasoned, not wanting to dwell too much on retrospection but rather enjoy her latest part of her unplanned adventure.

He stood up, then gestured for her to

sit down. 'I merely wished to make sure that you are all right after your ordeal, I am ashamed that a visitor to our country should have such a tarnished view of it.' He signalled for a pot of fresh coffee to be brought over for her. 'Please call me Adam.'

She made herself comfortable and relaxed into the cushioning of the rattan chair. 'You are originally from Malaysia then?' she asked, recognising the feeling of relief that she was not going to be sitting in another restaurant on her own.

'Yes, I was born here, but I have spent a long time in England and enjoy both cultures — benefiting from experiencing the best of both worlds. I am very fortunate.'

'You do not see the worst of those worlds then?' she asked by return, without stopping to ponder her question.

'I choose not to dwell upon the negative side of life and instead feed off the positive. It is my way of enjoying life.'

Jemma was impressed by his answer and the degree of humility he showed within it. It certainly was a refreshing change from listening to Luke moaning about how things were always wrong back home — everything from recession, taxes, war, weather, transport: his list of pet hates seemed endless. 'So, where do you live now?' She was not being nosey but was fascinated by this confident individual who still had the ability to appear genuinely modest at the same time.

'I have family still living in Kuala Lumpur who I visit twice a year, but have business in London where I spend most of my time. So, what about you, miss, are you here on holiday?' he asked, as he placed the fine porcelain milk jug down by her cup. 'It has been chilled and is from New Zealand so shall taste almost like English milk. This, not being a dairy country, means that outside such establishments you will find your coffee will taste differently from what you are used to and some of the local substitutes are very sweet, such as condensed milk or artificial ones.'

Jemma looked down and stared at the plate of untouched fruit. She sipped her coffee wondering just how much she should tell this stranger. 'You are a mine of information; this looks delicious,' she answered.

He looked at her plate, and then spoke quietly to her as if not to offend. 'You must eat, miss, or you will not survive the heat, it saps energy from you. I feel like I am addressing a teacher . . . miss.'

'Are you always this caring to strangers, Mr Li?' she asked him, then tasted the lovely sweetness of the papaya as it melted in her mouth, 'or just females who fall foul of muggers in the street?'

'Adam,' he repeated, 'and no, not really — well maybe if they're pretty,' he laughed and then blushed slightly, 'but it seems that we were meant to meet, so I believe your safety is now an issue of concern to me.'

'I was actually supposed to be meeting someone at that restaurant but they did not show up, or else I would not have been there on my own. I should have eaten in the air-conditioned restaurant here, safe and sound, but then our paths would not have crossed. However, as yet, my friend still has not arrived. I admit that I have yet to check at the reception to see if a message has been left for me, though. It is possible he was delayed and arrived late last night, I suppose.' She sounded totally unconvinced. 'My name is Jemma, by the way.' She ate her fruit then glanced at the pao, tantalisingly steaming as they were served onto the small plates and offered to the hotel guests.

Intuitively, he stood up, ordered a selection of small buns and siu mai and brought back a number of small plates to their table, placing one by her coffee before sitting back down.

'Please try them. Don't feel like you have to eat them all if you don't want to, just enjoy the experience.'

Jemma needed no encouragement. They were tasty morsels that she relished. She noticed as she picked one up in between her chopsticks that he was wearing a carved piece of jade on a strong gold chain. She slipped the small delicacy into her mouth and replaced her chopsticks upon their rest. His eyes met hers.

'It's beautiful,' she commented.

He looped the chain over his head, removing it from his neck and handed it to her for her to have a closer look at it. She took it from him carefully and saw that on one side of the jade was carved the figure of a dragon, whilst on the other was that of a phoenix. It was still warm to the touch and she felt as if he was sharing something precious and personal with her.

'Do they have a meaning or are they purely decorative, Adam?' she asked, as she carefully moved it around in her fingers, admiring the skill of the workmanship as the light highlighted the craft of the carver. It had not crossed her mind to view it as though assessing its obvious value. Carefully, she placed it on his folded and untouched napkin, which was still laid next to his hand. The gold and jade contrasted beautifully with the vanilla linen.

'Yes, they can have. In Chinese art, symbols often have meanings. Many have more than one. With the dragon and the phoenix, one representation is that of the empress and the emperor. That is just one interpretation.'

'Do you have an 'empress', Adam?' she asked without hesitation, and they both looked at the other silently for a moment, as if they were crossing some line. It was a personal question, yet he was no more than a stranger to her, but Jemma really wanted to know the answer. It was a very strange sensation. Jemma felt drawn to him and wondered if it was because he had acted like a hero and rescued her from an attacker when she was surrounded by strangers. He had been the only one to step out of the crowd and help her. Was this a sort of hero worship thing that she was feeling? It had happened at a time when her own relationship had fallen short of her hopes and ideals.

'No, not any more . . . her tastes were too extravagant for mine, so we have parted, before we made a lifetime commitment to folly.' He smiled politely, but this time his eyes did not sparkle.

'You miss her still?' she asked.

He shrugged and shifted a little awkwardly in the chair. 'I am sorry when relationships do not work out. Inevitably someone is hurt, and time is too precious for that. I prefer to be with people who are optimistic, who give off energy, not take it away from you with constant demands and complaints.'

She picked up her chopsticks, carefully balancing one of the steam buns between them. He was watching her, noting the confidence she had with them. Unbeknown to him it was due to a gift of a pair she had been given as a child from an aunt. She had played with them, using her bead set, patiently picking up each one in turn until she had mastered the unusual gift. It made her smile at the memory because then her life was so simple she could never have imagined going so far as London let alone Malaysia.

'The person you are waiting for, is he your dragon?' He smiled at his analogy, before eating his own pao.

'He is one, but not as you mean. In our culture 'dragons' have, I think, a different meaning — they breathe fire when angered. Luke is just a friend, now, and one who has some explaining to do once he does arrive.' She sipped her coffee and noted he was drinking what she guessed was jasmine tea. 'What is the business you have in London, Adam?'

He glanced at his watch. 'Miss . . . I mean Jemma, you must excuse me I need to make a phone call to someone about an order before they leave the office. I would love to speak to you again and continue our chat. Please finish your breakfast and if there is no message left for you offering profuse apologies, please phone me in my room 2014 and I will be pleased to show you around the city safely.' He stood up and left her.

She watched him walk away confidently, but not in the same manner as Luke strode along as if he owned the place; Adam seemed more centred, he owned his own space.

'Well, Adam Li,' Jemma thought, 'you are persistent but not pushy.' She refilled her coffee and was taking a sip, savouring the fine roast flavour knowing only too well that this was something she would only find in such places as the hotel. Then her eyes caught sight of the gold chain. He had knocked the napkin which had nearly obscured his chain from view. She reached out for it and studied the green jade pendant, now cold to her touch. Surely he would not forget something so valuable. She picked it up and looked for him but he was already nearly at the lift. Jemma smiled; she would have to return it to him now. She placed it in her pocket, finished her breakfast and then made her way toward the concierge. First she wanted to find out what Luke was playing at, hoping that there was no message left for her summoning her to meet him in another exotic and awkward place. She didn't want to be left waiting again; the memory of the pull on her bag strap and her falling on the open road made her shiver. Her confidence had taken a knock. If there was still no message then she would gladly take Adam Li up on his offer once she had returned the pendant to its mysterious owner.

She waited for the concierge to check with the reception staff to see if a message was waiting for her, when she heard the familiar voice behind her.

'There you are! I've been looking for you for over half an hour.' Luke placed a hand possessively on her shoulder as she turned around to face him.

'So was I — last evening, for

instance, but for more like an hour and a half, Luke, you left me waiting by the roadside!' Jemma snapped back at him, recognising that the strongest emotion she was feeling was not that of anger but disappointment because he was here. She had been determined to be cool, controlled and distant. Perhaps it was the strength of her disappointment which had triggered a feeling of guilt. He had finally turned up and that had stoked her angry response. Her hand was still holding the emperor and the empress pendant safely in her pocket.

He patted her shoulder in an almost patronising way then cupped her elbow, whilst smiling across at the pretty receptionist, and steered Jemma away in the direction of the lift. They stood facing the golden doors in silence, waiting for the delicate ping to announce the lift's arrival.

'Jemma, my flight was delayed. I couldn't help that and I couldn't let you know in time before you had left for dinner. I knew you wouldn't starve so I thought I'd catch up with you afterwards. But things got worse and there you are — I'm here now. That's what matters. Now what room are we in?'

He sounded as if he had made his explanation to her and the matter had been dealt with. Not that she agreed. 'So why didn't you meet me when you did arrive or leave a message with the hotel for me? By the way, we are not in a room. However, I am in 2012; you are in your own room whenever you book into it, I presume, as mine is for single occupancy only!' Jemma stared at him as his hand fell to his side and he picked up his leather holdall in the other as the lift pinged.

The doors opened, revealing a mosaic marble floor in the shape of orchids, contrasting with the natural wood walls. A large mirror on the facing wall seemed to mock them as they stared unhappily at each other as they entered. The fittings and hand rail were all made in a shiny gold colour. Heavy as her heart was she couldn't help but admire the beauty of this hotel. The details were carefully matched, made and finished to a high standard, no sloppy workmanship here. How different it was to the life on the street she had been in the previous night.

'You are being childish, Jem.' He stared at the panel of buttons with the porcelain numbers inlaid on each button. '2012, you say?' He pressed the button for floor two.

'My room is, yes, 2012,' she looked at him, 'and I am no child!'

The doors closed. She looked down, distracted by the pattern of the floor. Then she felt his arm grasp her around the waist as he scooped her up in his free arm and kissed her full on the mouth.

Jemma felt herself respond to his familiar embrace at first, but then, as her fingers gripped the chain and pendant still resting in her hand, she remembered the attack of the previous evening and pulled away.

He grinned at her. 'You know you've missed me. You're angry because we missed a night together. Come on, let me shower and we'll make up. I'll show you how sorry I am and explain what happened to keep me away from you over dinner.' He winked at her as the lift arrived at floor two. With a gentle movement the doors opened and he stepped out, looking for her room number. She wanted to shout at him angrily, 'I was mugged and you weren't there!' as if the two events were connected and it was his entire fault that she was targeted. But the words stuck in her throat and for some inexplicable reason she did not want him to know what had happened. It would be admitting she hadn't coped without him being around, and that she did not want to do. Also, she had met Adam Li and he was so different to Luke that she wanted to keep them apart. She was confused. She may never see Li again, but right now she wanted to take him up on his offer, but Luke had turned up.

'Has George phoned you? Has the sale been finalised?' Luke changed the subject as business and money entered his busy brain once more. 'I told George, my estate agent, to contact you here if there was any movement in the last two days. The money should be changing hands, Jem. I hope they are not going to mess us about because we're not in the country. Still, you'll be back at the end of the week and can jolly them up then. I'll be there after I've nipped to see a guy in Singapore. Shouldn't take more than four days to suss him out, but I don't want to leave things as they are at home any longer than needs be. You can sort out a cheap rental place for us for a month or two when you return to work. The more they delay in the transfer of funds the more interest we lose out on.'

He didn't stop to wait for her, but made his way to her room door. It was no more than she would have expected . . . unfortunately. Telling him she was not going back to the

UK for him or anyone just yet, was going to be difficult, not to mention the fact she had emailed her notice to her boss. She no longer worked for a bank, she had opted for voluntary redundancy and the date had been readily agreed. Her own funds were in the process of being transferred to her. She hoped the walls of the hotel were thick enough because the eruption was going to be of volcanic proportions when she told him. But beyond the row and the tears, there would be that beautiful word — freedom. The freedom to make her own decisions again, control her own money and see who she wanted to whether they were going to be a good contact or not. She wanted to have friends again that were just good people and not a business opportunity. The word 'networking' made her cringe.

She looked guiltily at room 2014 as she passed by, feeling the pendant still warm in her grasp. She should knock on the door straight away and return it to Mr Li . . . Adam, but not with Luke looking on impatiently, scowling at her disapprovingly. He was already holding his hand out for the key card.

'Jemma, none of the rooms in a place like this are single here and the rate is per room, not per person, so come on in. They all have at least one double bed. I'm tired and need to shower; it's bloody hot out there.'

She reluctantly walked to her own door and zapped her key card through the lock whilst promising her conscience that she would return the pendant to its rightful owner as soon as she had sorted issues out with Luke, and organised his own room. Right now she needed space — her own, and with it she hoped she would regain control of her sanity and life too.

4

Jemma closed the door behind her. Instantly the aura of her lovely room, with the fresh orchid laid carefully upon the turned back sheet of a made up bed, changed as he strode purposefully in. Instead of it being her temporary space, her freedom, it became like a gilded cage — a luxurious prison.

Luke flung his bag across the room so it landed on the chair by the window, as if taking control of the place — her own for a change, and as usual he was claiming it as his own. He sprang back onto the bed with an athletic fling, grinning at her, unaware that he had knocked the orchid onto the floor.

'Come here, Jem — don't be so distant. Let me show you how sorry I am.' He held his hand out to her expecting her to fall so easily into his arms.

48

Jemma knelt down on one knee by the bed and picked up the orchid. She placed it on the bedside table. 'You said you were sweaty and needed a shower, Luke. I think you should go ahead and have one before we talk, otherwise we shall both be distracted.' She looked at him impatiently.

She stood up, glancing back at his recumbent figure laid out on the bed and ignored his disgruntled expression. A dark look shadowed his eyes as once again she had not done as he had bidden her. This new behaviour of hers was definitely not pleasing him.

'I'll shower, whilst you sort yourself out, and then I shall talk to you if that is what you want. Jemma, I want us to work together. We have such a challenge in store, a future which offers a lot more than you ever thought you could earn in a bank, but we can't do it if you're going to have peculiar moods all the time. Think about it, you are behaving like a spoilt child. I need to rely on you, not have you mumbling on about one missed appointment,' he said pointedly.

'Appointment!' she repeated, folding her arms in front of her in disgust.

'Date then!' he growled. 'Same thing really.' He grabbed his toiletries bag and headed for the bathroom, slamming the door behind him.

'Oh, I've thought about it, Luke, in fact I've thought about nothing else all night. What is a 'date' to me, is an 'appointment' to you — what is fine to you, is a total disappointment to me, which left me vulnerable and in danger . . . ' She knew he could not hear her but she didn't care. 'I want you to talk to me, do I? No, Luke, I want you to listen!' The row was brewing like a storm building within her and soon the tornado would be released — a tropical one in magnitude. However, it was still to come. So she took the pendant out from her pocket and looked at it one last time in her hands before heading back out into the corridor. She so hoped she hadn't missed Adam Li. He may have gone back down to the restaurant to reclaim it. For all she knew he may have reported it missing to the staff at the front desk. How would she explain placing it in her pocket if she had been seen taking it from the table and had not made any attempt to return it to him? With great difficulty, was the only reply she could think of. No, now was the time to act. She was beginning to feel like a thief, albeit an unwilling one.

Standing outside room 2014 she pressed the bell and waited patiently with one eye watching her own room door in case Luke had heard her leave and was about to appear with a towel wrapped around his waist, asking her accusingly what the hell she was playing at. The scene played out in her mind and a smile crossed her face. How embarrassing that would be! Then realising she may be being watched, knowing that Mr Li would be looking at her through the fish eye peephole in the door, she dismissed all thoughts of Luke from her mind as she tried to act calmly, contented and not like a hormonal female who was about to have the row of her life with her ex lover.

The door opened and Adam Li stood there in a cream silk suit. The jacket with a mandarin collar hung open. The trousers were casually made for ease of movement, yet the suit was of good quality and hung beautifully as he moved position. She tried not to stare at his muscular chest and flat stomach, but she had not expected him to be dressed like this, although it was, she had to admit, a look which definitely suited him.

'Sorry, Jemma. I had decided you must not have had time for sightseeing so instead I changed ready to do some exercises. Please come in . . . ' He walked away from her, not seeing her hesitate in the doorway as she glanced back to her own. There was no audible noise so she took the pendant out of her pocket, held it in her hand and followed him to where he had a wooden tree-like object standing by the large window that looked over the city. She recognised it from martial arts films; she thought she remembered one in a documentary once.

'Interesting,' she said, as she inspected it curiously.

'I use it for training. I designed it myself for travelling. It comes apart and fits into a relatively small bag. I am thinking of marketing it. Just one problem that I haven't solved is that at the moment it is still not quite right. It gives a little too much after it has been used for some months, and I don't want to market something that will not last.'

'I'm impressed. You are a martial art's gadget designer?' She smiled knowing that she had no knowledge of anything to do with that world. The title was equally clumsy, but it was what he had described himself doing.

'Well, in a way you are nearly correct. Do you wish to go sightseeing now, Jemma?'

He was looking at her as if he was

sincerely hopeful that she would.

'No . . . I can't at the moment. My friend has arrived at last and I have some unfinished business to sort out with him. However, I had to return this before you started a search party for it.' She produced the pendant from her hand letting it sway carefully, then with a bold and equally careful act she stepped forward and placed it around his neck. It fell against his tanned chest. His eyes peered into hers. 'I thought there might be the police knocking at my door before long as I did not return it straight away, because I was distracted when my friend arrived. I had intended to, though.'

'Thank you for taking care of it, but I would not have organised a search party, because the waiter told me you had taken it with you for safekeeping.'

Her eyes widened, and she blushed slightly? 'You mean you knew that I had it all the time? What must you have been thinking of me?' She took a step back, suddenly aware how close she was to him, and also remembering the irate man who was refreshing himself in her own shower. How much more annoyed he would be if he knew she was in another man's bedroom. The thought had not really occurred to her in those terms until that moment but then in the last twenty-four hours life had thrown up a series of unexpected events.

'I thought you would return it to me when you could.' He smiled and folded his arms casually in front of him.

'You never doubted that I would . . . I mean it is beautiful and I could have so easily kept it?' she asked, not knowing why he should trust her.

'No, I didn't. You are not a thief. I am a good judge of character, I think.'

'No wonder you were quick to knock the man off the bike in the street. You are trained to attack people.' Jemma glanced at the wooden exercise tree.

He laughed. 'Actually, I train to defend people, but it can be reversed when needed. Would you like a drink, Jemma?' He pointed to the kettle and the ornate jar of oolong tea next to it.

She smiled as Luke would have pointed to the minibar. 'No, I think that now the empress and emperor are back in their rightful home I shall go, but thank you for the . . . well, thank you.'

'You are welcome,' he said as he walked her to the door.

As he opened it she looked at him for a moment, There was an air of anticipation hovering between them. 'Look,' she began, 'I owe you and would like to repay your kindness by buying you dinner tonight. Purely as a thank you.' She added a little awkwardly.

'You've thanked me enough but I shall be glad to accept the offer. If you meet me in the foyer at 7, I will take you to a place where you can sit in an air-conditioned room and relax away from prying eyes and the city traffic — and away from any street crimes, Miss Jemma Ward.'

'Fine, see you at 7 then.' She left his room and he watched her. She stopped and glanced back. 'How do you know my surname, Mr Li?'

He was standing with one arm resting on the door frame by his head. 'It was on the label on your rucksack,' he replied simply.

'Of course,' she answered, amazed at his observational skills as the label was quite worn and small. She pressed the lift button and the bell rang announcing the lift had promptly arrived. She would book Luke into a room on the seventh floor, which should be far enough away from her to allow him to recover from the infuriating new Jemma. Once that was done she would return to her own room and break the good news to him.

It was with this resolve she arrived back in room 2012 to find Luke using her laptop and talking on her phone to the estate agent in London.

If Jemma expected him to be pacing the floor anxiously waiting for her return, she was to be mistaken . . . as usual.

5

Jemma put his room key card down on the chair next to where his bag was. Without a word, and whilst he was preoccupied with his image in the mirror, she collected his toiletries from the bathroom, disgustedly picked up the wet towels from the floor and hung them over the towel rail. Fortunately there was another clean set on the shelf which she could use.

She then ventured back into the bedroom and returned his toilet bag into his leather holdall. The time for Mount Vesuvius to let off pressure had arrived. 'Control,' she said to herself, running the words silently through her mind, adding 'just keep in control of your temper, lose it and he won't take you seriously — as if he ever had!' It did not help.

She stayed a few feet away from

where he was standing. 'Luke, I want to talk to you and I want you to listen to me carefully. Then when you have heard what I have wanted to tell you for months, please go to your room, number 7210, and think seriously about what I have said to you.' At the mention of the other room number he finally looked at her, acknowledging her presence.

It was more of a stare really, the sort you would give a child who had misbehaved — badly. Wearing his jeans, no shirt and with his hair still wet, he looked strong and attractive, but not in the honed muscular and supple way that Adam Li had. Luke's appearance was more down to being a careful eater, and using the gym regularly. He knew he was pleasing to the eye on the outside, but Jemma's concern was what had happened to the person on the inside which had become less than attractive in her eyes.

'OK, Jem, tell me what's on your mind. Get it out of your system and let's clear the air. Then I shall tell you what I have found out is going on back home and what you will need to do when you return to London. You see, whilst you were out mooning around and costing us more money by booking unnecessary rooms, I've spoken to George and to the bank and have found out that the funds will clear by lunchtime tomorrow, then you can . . .'

'Stop it, Luke! Listen to yourself. I have just told you that I have something important to tell you, and you start off by ordering me about again telling me what you have been doing and what you want — expect me to do next. Well, I'm not going to do any of it. I'm not returning to London! I have no intention of being back in the UK for at least another four weeks.' She had forgotten her promise to herself of keeping in control. She had lost it and was now going for the eruption instead. One way or another, he was going to understand just how unhappy she was before he left the room. 'I'm not returning to my old job either and there is no 'we' anymore. 'We' are over. I've been trying to tell you for weeks that I can't stand your dominating — arrogant — suffocating, attitude. I want my own space, and I want my own life back whilst I still know who and what I am!'

She was practically shaking with pent up frustration. He was staring at her, lost for words, or so it appeared.

Then as if an explanation had entered his conscious mind, 'Are you — you know — pregnant?' he asked.

Jemma could see the horrified look of shock in his eyes as he forced the word 'pregnant' out of his mouth. 'No! I am not.'

'Thank goodness for that. For a moment there I thought your hormones had addled your wits. Now what is this about? Oh, I get it, you're not on your . . . '

'No, Luke. Not that either. My hormones are fine. My health is excellent and my sanity has never been clearer or my mind more focussed. It is you who is acting badly here, and you who needs to listen for a change. Luke, if we were married we would be talking about setting things up for a divorce, but as you never asked me to marry you in the first place, I don't need to have a divorce to separate from you. True, we need to sort out our financial affairs, yes, but otherwise we're free agents.' She swallowed. Somehow saying those words so bluntly threatened to undo her resolve. He almost flinched and she fought back the moisture that seemed to be wanting to escape from her eyes. It was the final admittance, that she, or rather 'they', had failed as a couple. She had always dreamed of falling in love, just once, and settling down after making a lifelong commitment. Her parents had, she could see nothing wrong with the idea, but it was not for her, not this time.

'Jemma, you know how to pick your moment, don't you? What we've achieved in four years will set us up for the next. We can now buy and rent out two properties in a cheaper area, north of the river perhaps, that is where the future lies. There is a recession coming, so now is the time to sell and soon will be the time to buy again when prices fall and repossessions hit hard.'

Jemma looked at him bewildered. She felt for people who lost their homes, whilst he saw it as just one more business opportunity.

'This isn't the time to be acting like a spoilt brat. This is for us! It is not the end of the adventure but the beginning. By the time we are ready to marry we will be living in our own private estate. Stick with me and I'll make it happen.' He placed his hands on her hips and tried to pull her to him, as if a kiss and a cuddle would make it all better and then she would dutifully and happily do as he wished.

'No, you don't see at all, Luke. I was ready. I loved our home. I never wanted to sell it. I thought we were making it ready for us, for a family, not to sell off. You changed. You decided to go for money, but I wanted the security and love of a family. No, Luke, we have been living separate lives with our own agendas without even knowing it.' She pulled away, standing by the door.

'You selfish bit . . . I would never have imagined you would pull a stunt like this. What is it really that's getting to you? Do you want to get your hands on your half of the profit? Is that it? Take the money and run? Don't you realise what we're doing? We're building a future . . . Or are you trying to force my hand and make me propose before I am ready to, is that it?'

'Castles in the sky. I don't want to live in a castle. I want to be free.'

His face and neck turned puce as he grabbed his bag. 'You better sort yourself out. I'll give you till breakfast tomorrow to think on it, then we either part as lovers, and you go to the UK or . . . Well, don't go down the opposite route, Jemma. I would strongly suggest you rethink just what you're throwing away.' He slammed the door shut behind him.

Jemma hugged herself, but beyond the tears that she felt bubbling up inside, there was a feeling of deep relief that she had finally said what she had wanted to for weeks, the burden had been heavy. She looked at the laptop and the phone. She had better call the bank and ask them how she can secure her half of the funds. It seemed a mercenary thought but he had threatened her. She had walked away from her job and now she would need to take care with the finances she was awarded from her redundancy and her half of the profits from the sale. If it had not been for her job in the bank to start with and the income, they would never have managed to buy their home in the first place, so she would secure her financial future for whatever lay ahead.

Once she replaced the phone she felt exhausted, collapsed onto the bed and slept soundly for what seemed like hours.

After the phone call and with a great

effort she forced herself to dress and take her swimming bag to the pool. It was an open air swimming pool on the eleventh floor with a landscaped water-fall, designed in an interesting irregular shape. It was beautiful, even to a mending heart. She had four hours left in which to be ready to take her 'have a go hero' out for a dinner. The thought brought her a feeling of hope that she would have a life beyond the cloud that Luke had cast over her.

Her senses were in a flux. This was the first date she had had with any male other than Luke for four years and she had chosen a complete unknown, in a strange land, at such a disturbing time. Perhaps her sanity was in danger of leading her into trouble again.

Jemma dived into the pool and gasped as the water was so cool in contrast to the steamy heat of the air around it. When she emerged in the bright sunshine at the other side of the pool she felt refreshed and invigorated — and alive.

6

By the time Jemma had returned to her room and changed, there were three messages waiting for her. The first told her to phone Luke's room, the second asked her to return his call as soon as possible. Finally, the third told her to join him for dinner so that they could talk things through. He suggested she be ready by 7 p.m., he would meet her in the lounge.

Jemma looked at her reflection in the mirror. It was 6.30 p.m. and she was already dressed in a chocolate coloured short-sleeved silk blouse which contrasted with her cream linen suit. Her bejewelled leather sandals were comfortable to walk in and cool to wear. Around her neck she wore a string of pearls that matched her drop earrings. With her auburn hair loose over her shoulders she felt fresh, and had tried not to think too much about her evening ahead as she had carefully prepared for it. Now, though, she had a problem, two evenings had been planned — one by her and the other by Luke. The problem had a name — which was Luke, and she thought that she had dealt with him for today, but, as usual, he was determined to have his way.

'What to do?' she asked her reflection. She sat on the edge of the bed, looked at the clock and thought — deeply. She did not want to make a scene in the lounge. However, neither did she wish to dine with him whilst trying to sort their lives out. Jemma thought that she had put her viewpoint over clearly and succinctly. She put her head in her hands. 'What to do?' she asked again, and then reached for the phone.

★   ★   ★

Down in the lobby Adam Li was ready for his unexpected, but welcome, date

68

and was casually browsing through the local newspaper when he saw the lift doors open. He looked over hoping it would be his new friend. Since the incident the previous evening, he had not been able to concentrate on his business, or sorting out his own differences with Ling. Instead, he had been preoccupied with the lovely lady who had so nearly been one more city crime statistic.

Instead of Jemma appearing, a man stepped out purposefully and approached the reception desk, clearly in a hurry.

'Has there been a message left for me?' He changed weight from one foot to the other as he placed his hands on the counter in front of the receptionist. He was tall, well built and Li could see the girl was looking intimidated by the man's build and manner.

'What is your name, sir, and your room number?' she asked politely, smiling at him nervously.

'Luke Stanton, room 2012 . . . I mean 7010.' He wrapped his fingers on the counter as he waited whilst she checked to see if he had any messages waiting.

Adam Li heard the room number and casually moved a little nearer the lift. He didn't like the look of the man and surmised that this was 'the friend' whom Jemma had unfinished business with.

'No, sir, there is no . . . '

'Are you sure?' he demanded to know.

'Yes, sir.' She shrugged almost apologetically.

'Phone room 2012 for me,' he ordered.

She dutifully phoned the room number. 'I am sorry, sir, the line is engaged.'

'Bloody hell!' He slammed a flat palm down on the counter top. 'I shall be in the bar, please try again in five minutes and have the call put through if she answers.' He stormed off.

Adam walked over to the counter. Smiling, he was about to speak to her and ask if he may try the room number when the moment was interrupted by another member of staff.

'Hey, that call was from room 2012 asking to tell the big guy, Mr Stanton, that she can't meet him tonight for dinner. Do you want me to tell him?'

'Would you?' the young woman asked, and the older one nodded, she looked quite pleased at being given the opportunity, unlike the younger receptionist, this lady was not at all intimidated by him.

Adam walked into the lift and pressed the button for floor 2. He hoped they did not miss each other. As the doors opened again, he was not to be disappointed as Jemma was standing waiting for it.

She looked a little nervous and surprised to see him.

'Hi.' He smiled at her and welcomed her into the lift. Instead of pressing L for Lobby, he pressed the button for floor 11.

'Mr Li . . . Adam, where are we

going?' she asked. The relief on her face was clear to see for they would not be crossing Luke's path. Wherever it was that Adam was taking her, it was nowhere near the lounge.

'Not far, Jemma. I wanted to make up for your downbeat meal yesterday. The restaurant here is excellent, air-conditioned and as the hotel links to a shopping centre, I thought that once we had dined we could go for a walk around the shopping mall before I return you safely to your room once more.' He looked at her. 'Is that fine with you, or would your prefer me to take you to a restaurant in the city?'

'That's fine, Adam. You are very thoughtful.'

The lift doors opened and two ladies dressed in golden silk cheongsam met them at a pedestal and welcomed them into the restaurant, 'The Golden Dragon'.

Jemma grinned at him. 'Excellent choice, Mr Li,' she said, as she was escorted into the restaurant and seated at a private table for two in a small bay at the edge of the dining area.

He did likewise. The menus were left and Chinese tea was served at the table.

'This is lovely,' she said, as she studied the gold carvings set against black marble on the wall.

'Good, enjoy it.'

Jemma looked at the exotic display of dishes listed in front of her and decided wholeheartedly as she looked back at Adam's friendly face, that she intended to do just that.

★   ★   ★

Luke was furious. He received the message and could have sworn the woman was laughing at him behind her cool persona. He stayed at the bar and ordered another Jack Daniels, it was whilst he downed his drink that his head swirled a little. He shook it to try to clear his mind and then realised it was his second and, as yet, he hadn't eaten. He looked at the barman. 'Do you serve food in here?'

'Snacks only.'

'I mean a meal, man.'

'No, sir, not in here. But there is a French cafe on floor 5, the salad and noodle bar in the basement or The Golden Dragon restaurant on floor 11.'

His stomach growled. He hadn't expected to eat alone and couldn't stand the thought that Jemma was undermining all that he had planned for the last four years. Why couldn't she back him up when he needed her to? He had brought her to the Far East and intended to show her sights she would never have seen, yet all she did was complain at him. It was unfortunate his schedule was delayed.

He sat upright on the bar stool and let out a low breath, then straightened his back and made sure he had his mobile in his pocket. He walked into the lift, admired his reflection in the doors as they closed, and pressed floor 11. He would phone her from the table and give her one last chance. If she still insisted on being standoffish and sulk like a child then he'd go to her room and settle it before the morning. One way or another she would return to England. No one walked out on him. No one would stop him from developing his plan, not even Jemma. Why couldn't she see it was as much for her as him? Eventually he would marry her, he might even want children, but not yet — certainly not now, a family would ruin everything they had. She just didn't understand what that was, but he would open her eyes and show her.

As he was greeted by two lovely ladies outside the restaurant he smiled charmingly at one and then the other. Perhaps, he wondered, if he should stay free. He knew they would respond and was not disappointed. Jemma just didn't realise how fortunate she was. If not for the financial ties he might just have considered the separation and let her go, but issues were involved. He needed her capital to reinvest with his to make his plan work, otherwise he was years off his target. He had to get through to her. Whatever the real reason for her outburst he would find out and, if it came down to an engagement ring, then perhaps he would have to invest in one. Yes, of course, that was it! He'd cracked it. Now for a good meal and then he'd go into the mall and choose one before wishing her a good, and peaceful night's sleep. He requested a quiet table and was led into the restaurant, admiring the view as he watched the slim figure in front of him slink along in her cheongsam, oblivious to the other customers already seated at the tables.

7

'Adam, I was wondering. If you have family in Kuala Lumpur, why are you staying here, in a hotel?' Jemma picked up a scallop with her chopsticks and felt the succulent morsel almost melt in her mouth. She could taste a hint of ginger which was so delicate it was a delight as it warmed her palate.

He grinned at her. 'I am here on business. I have already stayed two weeks at my sister's place with her family, and now I have my own space again whilst I prepare to return to the UK.'

'What is your business, Adam?' She sat back and watched him ponder her question. He was a mystery. There was gentleness to his manner, yet he would bring down a moving motorbike rider in flight without hesitation, which took some nerve and inner strength. When he had appeared at his room door it was as though he should have been on the set of a Hong Kong martial arts movie. Now, sitting in front of her, relaxed, he looked casual and unassuming, in a neat crisp white open necked shirt and brown slacks.

He looked directly at her. 'I am an interior designer.' Adam seemed to be studying her, as if watching for her first, immediate reaction.

'Really?' she sipped her jasmine tea and tried not to look surprised. 'I'm impressed.'

'I wondered if it would be an image which you would find hard to fit me.'

'Why? You have an eye for design and style,' she said and saw his expression change.

He smiled, obviously pleased with her answer. 'I have built up a clientele over the last six years and am pleased to say that the business has grown steadily.' He opened his wallet and produced a card. '*Living Spaces*' it read, embossed in gold with an elongated dragon at one side and a phoenix at the other. 'I am a guest in this hotel because I have just finished doing work for the manager. I have also been sourcing some fabric suppliers and accessories to ship back home to the UK. I like to work with both east and west influences. I find the two can compliment each other very well.'

'Did you go to university in London?' she asked, not missing the overtone his last comment held. She felt a tinge of jealousy creeping in, only in a very mild sense, as she would have loved to have gone to art college.

'I studied fashion at college and took it on from there. I have also worked for a firm of interior designers in London to build an understanding of the business and also to build my own plan for a future. So what do you do, Jemma?'

He gave her a card and she slipped it into her bag, pleased that she was in possession of an emperor and empress again.

'I did work for a bank. However, I have emailed my resignation to them by taking voluntary redundancy.' She looked down for a second, and then helped herself to some crispy beef. 'I've decided to have a gap month to travel, then go back and reinvent myself.'

'Where will you go for a month? Are you staying in Malaysia? What is your reinvention plan for yourself?' He picked up a satay stick, dipping it in the nutty sauce before expertly eating it without dripping one drop.

'I was thinking of going to Sydney, and then travelling down to Brisbane and on to the Gold Coast. I should be able to do that in the time and it will give me the space I need to decide what I want to do on my return. I always wanted to go to art school. I both envy you and admire you because you have followed your vision and made it a reality.' She tucked into a spoonful of the Malaysian chicken curry, loving the creamy coconut flavour.

'Is this something you have been

planning for a long time?' he asked, but she sensed that he already knew the answer. 'Envy is a very wasteful emotion, turn it into action and make your own dream come to fruition.'

'So wise!' she said, and he laughed. 'No, I've been thinking on it for only a couple of months. Before that I thought my dragon was wanting a long term relationship with his phoenix and was making a nest for a lasting future together. He was, but only on his terms, which made me think more deeply about what I actually wanted to do with my life.'

'Was he very dominant?' Adam asked.

'I used to admire his strength, his perception of what we should do to forge that future. The thing is he is always looking at the future and not appreciating where we are in the present. I know that it would be wrong to be totally blinkered by the present, but I can't live like that. Tomorrow will never come.' She dabbed a napkin to her lips and contemplated having Pak

Choi, which had been steamed then covered with a zig zag of oyster sauce.

'Didn't he want you to be a person in your own right?'

'Not really. Yes, I suppose he did so long as I agreed with and followed him.' She looked at Adam, surprised that she should be discussing her feelings so openly with him: revealing the details of her broken relationship with Luke, who was here in the hotel. So near to her, yet so distant in the manner of being there for her and here she was with a comparative stranger, having a lovely intimate dinner. 'So tell me about your ex, Adam. Why did she want more than you?'

'Greed,' he said simply and placed his chopsticks on their fish shaped rest.

'That simple?'

'Yes, unfortunately. She wanted me to move into a higher end market. Her father would place the capital there at my disposal so long as I used his accountant and married his daughter. The wedding would have been grand

and in Hong Kong where I would have had the main branch of my new empire opened.' He coloured slightly, his composure changing, replaced by a new emotion — hurt.

'You didn't want an accountant and a father-in-law running your business and life.'

'You understand perfectly.' He grinned at her and she smiled at him. Both had so much in common, yet their lives had been so different in many ways.

8

Luke was seated in a private bay in the restaurant. The table was set for two as he said a lady would be joining him shortly — very shortly, he hoped. There were five of these identical high backed leather upholstered bays at each side of the semi-circular restaurant. The larger round tables for groups and families were arranged on the main floor area. Each of the chairs was covered in a rich dark tapestry. Luke was quite pleased with his choice of seat, sitting so that he could view the entrance to the restaurant; from here he could hear the lift bell ping just beyond it. The booths were positioned at such an angle that they offered privacy to the diners. He liked that, he would soon win her round and make her see sense. She, he had decided, was making him pay for standing her up the previous evening.

Jemma had dared to stand him up at such a time, though. Hadn't he been more than fair? If it was because she had eaten alone in the Jalan that she was sulking, then she really was being childish. Surely she could cope with a few stares from the locals, for goodness sake. He reasoned that lots of women wanted to turn heads; if her richly coloured hair and slender build didn't raise a few eyebrows here, then where else would they? It wasn't as though the restaurant wasn't safe; it was only a street away from the hotel. She, he knew, was just being bloody difficult.

She was usually so unassuming, yet tonight she had treated him so coolly, being as a diva. Perhap, that was it, he wondered . . . She had turned heads and it had started to change her 'Women!' he muttered under his breath, casually pulling his mobile phone out of his pocket and also a small jewellery box. She was being very difficult at a time when he needed her — or needed her share of the capital and her connections at the bank. Either way, a few hundred ringit spent on a ring he had decided was a small price to pay to get his life back on track. Why should she kick up such a fuss now? He had always been careful to make sure she did not want for anything, taken her out every other weekend; he even let her choose the decorations and furniture for the house — despite the fact that he preferred minimalist decor to cushy and homely soft furnishings. She liked textiles, she had said; he didn't, but he had let her have her way.

He was quite sure that she had no idea about Trisha, his on-off ex. Just at the moment he was thinking of calling her to arrange a pleasant home-coming for him. He knew Trisha secretly wanted him back. Pretty she was, quite bright, but lacked that bit of class that Jemma naturally had. Nope, he would give Jemma one last chance, and if not — if she wouldn't come around and see reason — then Trisha's lucky day was about to dawn. She had a house that could be sold and then with his half of the sale of the place in Kent he was sure he could still move up the next rung of the property ladder. Trisha would do anything for him. Jemma just had no realisation of how much she could lose.

Trisha, he knew he could manipulate to sign anything, no doubt. But he preferred Jemma and didn't want to complicate life anymore by courting anew, it would be too costly in pounds, effort and time. He wanted to move on.

★ ★ ★

'Adam, how long ago did you split up from . . . ' Jemma smiled. She couldn't keep calling her after an ancient dynastic queen. It was silly, yet she had no real reason to pry into this man's personal life and ask anything of him, yet he fascinated her.

Reassuringly he smiled back at her. 'My empress 'in waiting' was called Ling. We broke up three weeks ago which is why now is a good time for me to catch up on my business issues over here and see my family.' He sat quietly whilst the table was cleared, then ordered something in Chinese.

'You ran away,' Jemma spoke quietly, even though the waiter had left them alone once more.

'Oh, so blunt, Miss Ward!' He feigned shock. 'Yes, actually you are quite right. I was not brave and bold. I did. A mugger is one thing, Ling in a temper is quite another. Although her name means delicate, her attitude when things are not to her pleasing, is far from it. I needed to regain my own space. I was tired of being told what I should do with my own business. If you have a vision for a future and when you include someone else in your life it is important that you can both work towards the same agreed goal. With Ling, she asked her father and then it was agreed what should be done. Suddenly my dream was their opportunity and all I could see was a nightmare before us.'

'So in a sense we are in the same situation. Both of us were at odds with what our partners imagined or planned for our futures.'

Adam nodded, 'Yes, I suppose we are.' He fidgeted with the gold napkin ring. 'Besides . . . ' He hesitated.

'What?' she urged.

'I was educated in the west and think more like a westerner than someone from a traditional family background. I think we saw things from different perspectives.'

Jemma saw his cheeks flush a little and found it quite charming.

'Do you think that is the worst chat-up line you have ever heard?' He shifted a little uneasily on his seat, for the first time showing a crack in his otherwise confident manner. 'I wouldn't say such a dumb thing to try to persuade you that I am not what I may appear to you to be — I am proud of being . . . '

'Adam, you don't need to explain what you are or are not to me. I can see what you mean. I don't box people in by sweeping them into categories. What you have said is not anything to be either proud or ashamed of; we are all what we are because of our past. We should embrace that as it has created us.' She was going to say more, but he seemed distracted for a moment as he stared toward the reception area of the restaurant. Jemma had heard the lift ping vaguely in the background, but from where she sat she could not see the people come and go, unlike Adam. 'Someone you know?' she enquired, feeling as though she wanted to turn and stare at whoever it was, to see if it was a lovely exotic lady, possibly by the name of Ling, who had entered, but she was far too polite to do so. Besides, she reasoned, that would stretch the boundaries of probability too far.

'No, just someone I passed in the lobby downstairs before we came up here. No one important, I'm sure.' His temporary loss of confidence evaporated. 'So tell me, how long since you parted from your dragon?'

He was watching her carefully. Again she thought she saw humour in those eyes, but she wasn't sure. She was almost too embarrassed to admit the truth but felt she should. After all this was not a date; it was more of a meal between two new friends.

'Three, officially, maybe four.' She shrugged and glanced at the larger tables, now filling up with family groups.

'Years, months, weeks — or days?' he was grinning at her.

'Hours,' she admitted quietly.

'Oh good! For one horrible moment I thought you were going to say minutes!' he laughed. 'You are still rebounding then?' Adam leaned forward slightly and with a gentle and natural gesture stroked her hand.

'In a way, but I am not looking for another attachment. I also want to make my own decisions in life and rediscover myself. Living with a dominant partner can become suffocating. I am not on the rebound, but I am in a new phase of my life. Luke will not let go of me easily and I have financial issues to sort out with him over the sale of our joint home.'

Jemma had no idea why she should tell this man so much.

'Will he try and cut you out of your share?'

Adam's attention was full on her as if it mattered to him. It was as if two souls were supporting each other's plight. 'He can't, even if he wanted to. Everything is going through the bank where I used to work. I have already taken legal advice and have issued clear instructions regarding my share of the profit. I'm afraid there is no reversing our split unless I revoke that. It is final. When he realises I have taken the initiative over the funds he will never forgive me for not asking him first. Of course, if I asked he would never have agreed.' Staring into his eyes, she sensed an understanding and he nodded.

'He won't take it easily. In fact he wanted to meet with me tonight, take me for a meal and, I suppose, try to change my mind. But I had another commitment.' She shrugged.

'You turned him down and kept our date?' He was genuinely humoured.

'You find that funny?' She flushed slightly, not seeing anything humorous about what she had just shared with him and also noting the term date.

'Yes, in a way, I do, but not quite in itself, not the way you think I mean. I . . . ' He sat forward as if he was going to divulge a secret when there was a gasp from one of the other diners. A waiter was carrying a tray on which a bowl was giving off clouds of dry ice as he crossed the floor to present this winter-wonderland platter of tropical fruit.

Jemma's eyes lit up like a child and she almost squealed with glee. Eyes turned to watch the display, taking in the scene until the air returned to its normality and then the family were then left to eat the chilled fruit in peace.

After her initial excitement had subsided she took a moment to compose herself, remembering her unanswered question. 'So why is it funny?' she repeated.

'Well, if I share something with you, please don't overreact . . . ' he began to explain as her phone rang, making her nearly drop a slice of star fruit from her silver fruit fork.

'Sorry,' she said, and reached in her small bag for her phone.

'Switch it off, Jemma, please trust me and continue — finish the meal undisturbed.'

The noise became louder as it was ignored. Another customer looked around so, instead of retrieving her call, she switched her phone off.

'Explain, Adam,' she said, and stabbed a piece of dragon fruit with her dessert fork.

9

Luke listened to the phone ring. It sounded at first as though it was gaining an echo as the ring seemed to become louder, but he thought it must have been the acoustics of the room playing with his hearing. He watched, slightly impressed, as other diners watched as a platter emanating dry ice was brought to a booth next but one to his own. 'Posers,' he muttered, as he strummed his fingers on the table impatiently. A waitress came for his order but he brushed her away with a wave of his free hand, starving hungry as he was. Jemma had better come to the restaurant quickly and stop being so selfishly childish. Then the unthinkable happened — the signal was lost! It stopped ringing. He phoned again but was told her phone was switched off. He thought it was a mistake, a loss of connection. They both were using local pay-as-you-go sim cards so there should be no operating difficulties. He used speed dial and tried one last time.

He was completely dumbstruck. Anger filled his every pore. Surrounded by people enjoying themselves, he was alone, jealous, and hungry. Never had he felt so abandoned in his life, or so rejected.

The waitress came back and smiled hopefully at him.

He ordered his food — in fact he ordered quite a lot, and a bottle of Jack Daniels. He needed to think this through before he presented himself at the door of room 2012, with the ring and his ultimatum. See if she would turn a diamond ring down, if that was what she craved so much. No one treated him in such a cavalier fashion. No one!

★ ★ ★

'Jemma,' Adam continued. 'Please don't stand up or look around but I believe the man who just phoned you . . . your dragon, is sitting three booths away from us right now.' He raised his eyebrows, but did not smile.

'What! Luke is in here? Phoning me . . . he hasn't seen me, has he? No, of course he would not be able to. If he had, he would be here accusing me of having an affair or some such.' She flushed slightly as Adam raised an eyebrow. 'He is an unreasonable man.' Jemma glanced instinctively over her shoulder knowing she would only see the back of the booth behind her yet still could not help the instinct. Lot's wife came to mind. Fortunately, she did not turn to a pillar of salt.

Adam winked at her. 'You lead an interesting life, Miss Ward. I was just starting to become bored here, separated from my own dramas as it is the last few days of my trip. Contemplating what will await me back home in London. Then you popped into my path and somehow things have not just been the same, life has become interesting to the point of intriguing.'

'What am I to do now?' She sighed. 'He is sitting between me and the exit. We are nearly finished our meal and he has just arrived. How do I leave this place without him seeing me and him making a scene?' She looked at him imploringly. Jemma had no wish to involve or embarrass Adam as he had been a good friend to her and she did not want to cause him to lose face.

'You could stay a little longer with me. Have you tried their speciality coffees? They are said to be one of the best in KL.' He asked for another look at the menu.

'I'm so full,' she admitted.

'I am in no hurry to leave yet, are you?' He looked at her hopefully.

'No, I guess not,' she decided, and chose one of the exquisite coffees based on Irish Whiskey thinking how strange it was, this cross cultural meal was turning out to be bizarre yet fantastic. At the same time she was praying that Luke didn't see her and make a scene.

Then realisation dawned. Whatever would he think if he saw her in a secluded booth with a stranger, another man? Especially, when she had broken things off with him that same day and moved money from their joint account. He would never understand, he would never even listen to her reason. How could she explain how she had made another male friend so quickly when she didn't understand herself. Luke didn't know about the bag snatcher or Adam's bold rescue. Or that what she had told him today had been on her mind for nearly three months, but he had been too busy to make time for her and listen.

Jemma decided that if she could stay calm and not panic, worse come to worse, she would walk straight out of the restaurant and face him in private most likely in her room. 'Poor Adam,' she said.

'What?' he laughed.

'Sorry . . . I was thinking out loud. 'One step removed from lunacy, I understand. It's just that if Luke makes a fuss like he is capable of, he won't listen to you or me whilst I explain how I came to be here with you.'

'Then you should say, 'Poor Luke', for if he makes a scene I shall escort you away from it, or restrain him if he became physically abusive. Either way, the shame would not be on me, or you, would it?'

His confidence had returned. Jemma watched her coffee arrive, carried carefully upon a tray. It looked, like everything else this evening, absolutely divine. They had even melted sugar around the rim of the glass so that it had a sweet edge to the richness trapped already within it.

'Still, I have involved you in my personal troubles and you are here on business of your own — with your own issues to sort out. Sorry, Adam, I seem to have brought you trouble,' she added quietly, and sipped her drink, letting the warmth wash through her after the contrast of the chilled fruit.

'No, I have involved myself — willingly. Let me take you out for the day tomorrow, away from him and your troubles.'

'I would love to say yes,' she admitted, but already felt guilty. As she sipped the last of her drink it was not the only thing she was feeling. The warmth was making her feel just a little light headed. She was sure it must have been a generous measure of the whiskey.

'Stay still!' Adam said abruptly, but then calmly sat back on his chair. He signed the chit for the bill to be added to the account for room 2014.

'No, this was to be my treat,' she began to protest, but he quickly placed a finger to his own lips, asking her to be quiet. She did so, but felt like a child being rebuked until Luke walked straight past their booth. She was so close she could have reached out a hand and touched his. He was heading for the men's room at the end of the restaurant. The toilets were discreetly hidden from view by a gold and black laminate wooden screen depicting birds of prey flying amongst a mountain scene.

'We leave now, Jemma.' He took her hand and led her away to the lifts.

'I feel dishonourable.' She looked at Adam as the doors closed. From holding her hand he now had one arm around her waist. It felt comfortable, warm and right. 'Running away,' she added.

'Only to fight another day, but not tonight, no fighting today!' He leaned his head on hers for a moment as the doors opened on the aisle to the shopping mall. 'Let's walk dinner off and I shall show you around this place without you being in danger of attack.'

'Why not?' she said, as her senses gathered and she let herself be led from the lift, hand in hand with her new friend, Adam.

10

Luke swayed as he waited for the lift to take him to floor 2. His reflection in the large mirror at the back of the lift showed an unsteady figure, trying to look proud. His head was held high, his back was straight but the legs bowed slightly. He had what was left of the Jack Daniels still in the bottle, which he carried in his hand, swinging it slightly as if the liquor remaining offered reassurance. His other hand was deep in his pocket holding the box that encased the engagement ring. He had a firm grip on this. It was precious, it had cost him money he had not planned to spend, he hadn't time to search around and equally bargain the price down, but he was sure that it would make her see sense. Luke felt a little queasy at the thought of actually going ahead with this move, but 'Hey!' he told himself out loud, these days it was not a legally binding contract and there was no time constraint between announcing your engagement and then marrying. 'What the hell, live dangerously.' He laughed at his guile, he was happy to be in a permanent state of being engaged, as opposed to actual marriage. Marriage threatened stability and the threat of children. Luke didn't want that yet, he wanted to build his little empire. He wanted to be free of a day job and, instead, manage his investments. He wasn't sure if he really wanted children at all, they drained you in every way and then left home. Not for him.

He stumbled out of the lift and used his hand to guide him along the hotel corridor by tracing the wall, stopping only to read the numbers on the doors. '2014, nope not that one! 2013 . . . Blast it, so near . . . 2012 . . . Got you my baby, now prepare to be stunned! Let's see who goes down on one knee now, eh?' He mumbled to himself deciding it would make a good, humble pie approach if he rang the door bell, then balanced on one knee whilst holding out the ring in his hand. He pushed the button, then slowly sank down, using the bottle of Jack Daniels to steady himself as the floor became closer; he assumed the traditional position of what he called a love struck fool. He was trying so hard; he hoped she would realise just how much. Trisha would not have been such hard work. Only the door didn't open, and the button was now a long way from his hands, which were full anyway with ring and bottle, so instead he sank back slowly onto his haunches, turned to face the lift and rested his back against the door. He would wait for her to come back from wherever she was hiding. I bet she's in the pool, he mused. He had fourteen hours before he had to take her to KLIA and put her on the London flight. He smiled, it would be a tender parting moment, he pictured her tear stained face as he waved her off, and she glanced down at her finger, content with her world and happy to go ahead with his plans. He smiled, he understood women. With that thought he closed his eyes, visualising the bittersweet departure over and over in his mind, only to fall into a deep and drunken slumber, as he sank down onto the floor.

★ ★ ★

Jemma was fascinated by the myriad shops and stalls which Adam showed her, but after a couple of hours, reluctantly they returned to the hotel.

The lift was quiet as Adam and Jemma stood either side, each leaning on the hand rail looking at each other. It had the feeling of anticlimax hanging in the air, like the feeling she had as a child at the end of a brilliant holiday when you don't really want to return to the familiar routine of school. However, the familiar for her was no more. Her world had changed. As she looked at Adam, she realised something within her had. That was what she thought until they stepped from the lift and saw the recumbent figure fast asleep outside her door — snoring.

'Oh, no!' Jemma ran over to him. 'He looks like a tramp!'

'I don't think so, not in a suit like this one.' Adam assessed the bottle, checking the level of the fluid inside it. 'But he would pass convincingly as a lush . . . ' His critical words sounded harsh. He paused and looked up at her adding, 'Possibly.'

'What to do, though, Adam? If I leave him here he could be reported and thrown out of the hotel. If I ask them to help me move him the same could happen.' She looked at Adam who was sitting in a squat position by him. Disdain showed openly on his face.

'I shall take his shoulders. Leave the bottle here. You could ditch it when you return; you lift his feet. We shall half carry, half drag him to his room. I don't want him left in there with you in this state. An angry man who has been drinking is not a good combination. Mind, if we're seen on CCTV we may get arrested for attempted murder or something — it will look very strange.' He opened his eyes wide and his mouth curled slightly at one side. 'The adventure continues, Miss Ward.'

'Thanks, you are coming to my rescue again.' She saw him glance at her but his thoughts were on the task in hand. He slipped his arms under Luke's and heaved him up by wrapping his arms around Luke's chest. Although Luke was taller, Adam was strong and showed little effort. Jemma lifted Luke's legs by looping his knees under her arms and supporting the weight by holding her own hands together. They waddled back to the lift which, fortunately, had not gone anywhere, and nearly threw him in as they swung his weight forward using gravity to their advantage. Even the slight jolt of landing on the floor did not wake him up.

'Not a perfect end to an otherwise

perfect evening,' she said.

'It was, wasn't it?' Adam replied, letting her step in first.

The doors opened as they arrived at floor 7. Luke, oblivious to what was happening, had assumed a foetal position upon the floor. Both Jemma and Adam popped their heads outside and looked left and right to see if anyone was coming. They caught each other's eye contact and grinned. 'This is like some sort of farce,' Jemma remarked as she resumed her knee carrying hold.

With relief they found his room was not too far away and placed him on the floor by his own door, whilst they caught their breath.

'The key?' Adam said. 'I'm not going through his pockets, Miss Ward. I don't rummage through guys' clothing.'

She grinned at him as he deliberately sounded prim, folding his arms in a resolved fashion as he waited for her to find Luke's key card. She tried his wallet first — it wasn't there; then she tried his inner pockets — no, nothing there either, then she searched his outside pockets. She pulled out his mobile phone, then found his card, which she passed to Adam, but as she put the mobile back, his hand rolled onto the floor revealing the ring box. Jemma stared at it and was instantly filled with guilt. She knew what it was. It had to be a ring, an engagement ring. She swallowed as she picked it up.

Adam had opened the door. 'Great, we can leave him on his bed and he won't remember a thing.' He glanced down at her and saw what she was staring at. He looked slightly crest-fallen. 'Should we?' He gestured into Luke's room.

'Yes, of course.'

After a few moments of heaving and lifting their sleeping burden they rolled him onto the bed.

Adam stepped back. 'Job done! We should leave. I don't really want to meet the guy if he wakes up with a head full of Jack Daniels.'

Jemma was still holding the ring box in her hand. The temptation to open it was great.

'Well?' his voice cut across her thoughts, 'Are you staying?'

'No, it's just that he had this in his hand.' She held her hand open letting the deep red box sit upon it.

He did not look impressed. 'Are you going to open it?' he had folded his hands across his chest again.

'It could be an engagement ring — he had it in his hand, Adam.' She was looking for inspiration, but saw only a blank face.

'Yes, he did, and he held a bottle of whiskey in his other one. You didn't mention how romantic the guy could be.' He had answered honestly and without hesitation.

Jemma almost winced.

'I'd better go.' Adam started to walk out.

'Wait, please.' She placed the box back in Luke's hand and then left with Adam.

He was quiet and ill at ease with her after what had been a really fun evening. 'You're right, Adam.'

'How so?' he said, as he stood outside his room.

'About Luke.' She glanced at the floor where minutes before her 'ex' had been in a drunken slumber completely out of this world, with a suspected engagement ring in his hand. 'He is not really romantic. This was wrong of him. He doesn't normally get drunk. Adam, I think he needs me.'

Adam's eyes did not betray any emotion. He merely left her with a question she had already asked herself. 'Jemma, I have enjoyed this evening very much except for your friend's futile display. He may need you, but Jemma, do you really need him? Especially if he behaves like that at such an important time as proposing to marry a beautiful and gentle woman.'

She was going to say something in his defence, out of what she knew was a misplaced loyalty, but Adam's words had such sincerity to them that she could not form a response that seemed adequate.

He kissed her lightly on her lips, preventing her from speaking. She was taken completely by surprise, both at his action and at her own natural response to him.

'Don't give your answer to me; the answer is for you and him . . . not me. I hope our paths cross again, Miss Ward.' He opened his door and she took two steps back then swiped her own key card through the lock and entered her room.

She flopped down onto the bed and stared out of the window looking at the night view over the city. Then her eyes caught sight of a card envelope left on the coffee table. She picked it up and flicked it open. It was as she had guessed — her ticket to London for a 10 a.m. flight in the morning, left, of course, in her room earlier in the day by Luke. It was what he wanted her to do, even if it meant marrying in order to have her do as he bid.

Did he really love her, but had not

found it easy to show it? She smiled; perhaps his way of showing his true feelings for their future was to build her an empire, castles in the sky. Why could he not realise she would be happy with a lot less. So what to do now? She touched her lips with one finger.

Guilt crept back into her mind as she thought of the man two doors away; remembering the feel of the stolen kiss. She wanted to see him again, not sure why, but he made her feel happy and free, yet respected and valued. With Luke, she just felt that she was taken for granted. Remembering the instructions she had sent immediately to the bank after she had told him her intention to leave him, she felt like a traitor, then there were her own plans to go to Australia. She sat down again, completely confused, completely torn between a sense of loyalty, a sense of adventure and another area of senses which was totally new and exciting and involved Adam.

11

Adam had an uneasy night. He usually slept deeply and woke early. Until two days ago he had his world planned out. Ling had been a frightening experience. She had been so delicate to the eye, unassuming by nature, or had appeared so, until they had dated for a few consecutive weeks. Once he had been introduced to her father it was as if he had given the man the right to a stake and share in his future — and business. He wasn't content with the level at which Li worked. He knew how to make it bigger and the return greater. All Adam had to do was accept handouts and move his main office to Hong Kong, whilst marrying the beautiful Ling and making her very happy. The man had not stopped to wonder why Adam worked and lived and loved London. It was that simple;

he was free there to find his own way. The life of an accountant which his own father had insisted he train for just was not for him. it crushed him. The burden of expectation for him to perform as a good and dutiful son was too much for him. He had not escaped from one domineering father figure to succumb to the will of another. Now, after years apart, he and his father respected and understood each other, but Adam had had to prove himself first and that had taken over five silent years. The rift was now healed and the love stronger for it.

He had moved on, leaving Ling in no doubt he would not return to her, no matter how many threatening calls her father made to him. He had even stayed in the hotel for five days to give himself some space, and picked up some work in the process.

Then just as everything was starting to settle down, the redheaded woman had crossed his path. He didn't want to be drawn to a female for some time, or so he had thought, but this lady was somehow different. She had appeared to him like a lost soul, and seeing her so frightened on the street after the bag snatch, he'd felt extremely drawn to her and her plight. He certainly didn't like the arrogant 'friend'. Adam sensed she deserved better. There was no harm in making a new friend.

He gazed out of the window. She was going to Australia and he was flying back to London. He wasn't sure if he would be her 'type', but she was warm with him and he trusted his own intuition. It was time to pick up his business again. He wished he was free to take off with Jemma and explore a different land and a new culture with this new and delightful lady.

He hit the wooden exercise tree with his forearm and shook his head; time to pack it up and move on. If fate wished that their paths would cross again then they most surely would. He never doubted that she would think twice before returning to her old life after seeing that man, Luke, in such a pathetic state. If she didn't then he had misjudged her, and his judgement was something he prided himself on being good.

He packed his bag, and as a last minute thought, slipped one of his cards under her door. On it he had written a simple note: 'Whenever, wherever, just phone. A L x'.

Luke woke up early after having a long and deep sleep. His head felt heavy but not too bad. Boy, had he drowned his sorrows the previous evening. He took two tablets after a cool shower, reckoning that if they mixed with the remnants of the Jack Daniels they'd work wonders. Luke stretched, he had to freshen up. Jemma must not know how pathetic he had become through the effect of the Mr Jack Daniels experience. She had never seen him in such a state and it just wouldn't do their relationship any good if she did now. Jemma had to respect him and follow his advice; she needed to feel she could trust him in company again. He laughed as he remembered the last time Trisha had seen him out of his head. It had been fun, but then she was different, she was regularly out of it.

He thought hard and remembered going to Jemma's room. He remembered kneeling down by the closed door. He groaned at that memory, then nothing. There were no memories of how he returned to his bed. Yet he had managed to make it back to his own room, waking with the ring still in his hand. At least he hadn't made a complete botch of things. He still had the ring and he knew she hadn't seen him. Therefore, he still had the time and would be sensitivity itself as he coerced Jemma into packing up and getting on that London flight. He would phone the bank as soon as that was done and make sure all the funds were available to use. He would then contact the estate agents and tell them to go ahead with the offer on the next two properties. He winked at himself in the mirror; life would be good again, he was sure of that; you just had to believe in yourself.

★ ★ ★

Jemma awoke early. She had slept well. Her head was clear and her heart felt lighter than it had for weeks. It struck her how amazing it was that the bleakest of problems can start to sort themselves out after a good night's sleep. She would shower, dress and pack. Then she would leave a contact number under Adam's door. Next she would breakfast and then wait for Luke to make contact with her as he surely would. It was going to be interesting to actually hear what he had to say for himself. Then she would tell him what she intended to do next.

★ ★ ★

Adam closed his door behind him. He carried his suitcase and sports bag with him; one in each hand and a flight bag slung over his shoulder.

Once outside in the corridor he placed his bags on the carpeted floor and took out the card from his pocket. As he bent down to slip it under the door, it opened.

He looked up at Jemma who was almost laughing at him because she had been going to nip to his door and slip her own mobile number under it.

He stood up quickly and both could not help but grin at each other.

'Did you think you had another drunk at your door?' he quipped.

'No, Mr Li, I think you are too cool and together to be seen in such a state.' She could see that her answer pleased him.

'I am impressed at your powers of discernment. However, I wanted you to have this as sometimes fate needs a little helping hand.' He handed her the card, which she read.

'I wanted you to have this.' She handed him a card bookmark on which was written John Wesley's Rule. It was one of her little mementos which she took with her when she travelled, not really knowing why, until she had met Adam. On the reverse she had written her mobile telephone number.

He looked at it intrigued, then read out the words, 'Do all the good you can . . . By all the means you can . . . In all the ways you can . . . in all the places you can . . . at all the times you can . . . to all the people you can . . . as long as ever you can. He sounds like he was an interesting guy.' He placed it within his wallet.

'Yes, he was.' She looked at the cases. 'You're checking out today too.'

He shrugged. 'I have a business to see to and issues to face. I'll try and be good, though.' He smiled at her impishly.

'You can't run from problems, they'll find you out. None of us can.'

The lift pinged and the doors opened. Luke stepped out, he looked taken aback when he saw Adam talking to Jemma at her door.

Adam's smiled disappeared. 'You were saying?'

'Timing is everything,' Jemma spoke quietly, then shook his hand. 'Goodbye, Mr Li, and I shall certainly contact you if I need my living spaces revitalised.'

There was a twinkle in her eye that Adam acknowledged. He turned away from her, nodded to Luke in a polite gesture of greeting, picked up his bags and disappeared into the waiting lift.

'Who was that?' Luke asked.

'Mr Li. He owns an interior designer business in London.' She stepped back into her room, letting Luke follow her. She was all packed up and ready to go, as soon as she had breakfasted and sorted things out with him.

'They shouldn't let them tout for business in a place like this!' He shook his head in disgust. 'Never mind him. We have to talk, Jemma. I think we have both been a little churlish. I thought long and hard about things last night and well . . . ' He gave her a hug. 'I've come to a decision that I know you'll like.' He kissed her tenderly on the lips then sat her down on the bed next to him.

Before she could speak, he placed the ring box in her hand. 'Here, this is for you.'

'What is it, Luke?' she asked.

'Isn't it obvious?' He looked a little taken aback. 'It is what you want.'

She raised an eyebrow. He had to say it, and he had to ask her. What type of a man was he?

'Jemma,' he opened the case for her and showed her the diamond ring, 'I know things could have been better between us. I want to be a better partner. Jem, accept this engagement ring and wear it with pride, and we'll start again.'

12

She looked at the gem stone glistening in the light that was shining through the large window. It was a decent size, dazzling within its gold claw setting; yet it was actually no more or less than a piece of the earth, ripped from its natural state and presented in a different form. Beautiful — only about six months too late for its appearance to have the impact upon her that Luke had expected.

If his emotional delivery had been more compelling, or sincere, she might have been persuaded to accept it there and then, believing his words, whilst throwing her arms around him and accepting his offer with all her heart — but that was what was missing — the heart of the actual proposal. Also, she had the image in her head of him outside her room door the previous evening lying in a drunken stupor. He obviously had no memory of this, or fortunately of the disgust that had shown upon the face of Adam Li.

'Luke, I am touched that you have made such a generous gesture but we need more than this to sort out the problems which have come between us.' She tried to sound gentle, appreciative and sincere. Jemma had never let down anyone before in the sense of breaking up a relationship. Luke was her first true love and admitting it was not all she had imagined it to be, hurt — like admitting to yourself you failed in some deeply personal way.

'You want more than this? It's an engagement ring, Jem! What has got into you? We haven't the time to book a registrar . . . ' Her surprise must have shown as he quickly continued . . . 'or priest and honeymoon here and now. Be patient, first things first. Let's do it in the right order. We have our whole life ahead of us, no need to rush it, is there?' He sat next to her, running his fingers gently through her hair.

The irony in his words was lost on him. In the correct order; she supposed his 'right order' was to meet a pleasant enough looking woman, live together, buy a family home, sell said home, have an argument then become engaged and buy more property and start all over again — always working towards the next goal and the distant wedding which had an ethereal quality attached to it rather than a tangible present. 'Yes, it is, but you haven't proposed to me properly, have you?'

He was speechless; he waved his hands around but there was not a response coming out of his mouth, which was very unusual for him. Luke appeared to be tongue-tied.

'I know why.' Jemma thought she would help him out.

He looked at her with a slightly bewildered stare. 'You do?'

'Yes.' She placed her hand on his, wrapping his fingers around the ring. 'This was a spur of the moment decision made through a haze of Jack Daniels. It has not been done with a clear head or a sincere heart. We need to step back from each other and take time out to think again about our futures and where we go next.'

Jemma thought she saw a flash of relief cross his face. 'So you want a little thinking time for us to sort our heads out and then start again . . . Fine, I can go with that.' He glanced around, not making any acknowledgement as to how she knew about the Jack Daniels. 'Look, I'll take you to KLIA and we'll check you in. Whilst you're on the flight you can look over these.' From his jacket pocket he pulled out an A5 envelope which held some folded A4 documents. 'They are the papers for the two cottages that I want us to make an offer on, but Jemma they'll go quickly and I know they are too good to miss. Imagine it, we live in one and rent the other on a six months lease, and that will pay more than the mortgage on both. We renovate as we live within one.

Once the winter is out, and the lodgers finish the lease, we can renovate the other and sell them in the spring. Brilliant isn't it? Some of the time I will have to be away on jobs but you can hold the fort. They are near the connection for the Liverpool Street line into the city so no problem there. You will be so near to your bank that it will save you so much travelling time from when you used to go in from Kent.' He was smiling and waving his hands about enthusiastically, yet all she could feel was a gaping chasm between them.

'Jemma, I won't be back for a week as I have to see a chap in Singapore to do with my work. It's a pretty big project I'm involved in, but when I come home we can do the whole down on one knee thing in style. We can go to Paris for a weekend, do the whole romantic bit.' He cupped her face in his hand and looked straight into her eyes. 'You deserve that, at least.'

He was so pleased with himself she almost felt sorry that she was about to blow his plans skyward. Luke had a really good job, so had she, yet he always wanted more. She wondered if he would ever be satisfied, and if not then why not? Ambition was a good thing but not everything, not to her anyway. That thought made her feel like it was her failing.

'Luke, you are not listening to me. I will change my plans and return to London instead of travelling on to Sydney . . . ' She knew he wasn't listening properly to her.

'Great . . . ' he enthused then repeated, 'Sydney?' He was puzzled and was about to hug her, but she stepped away from him.

'But I am returning to sort out my own affairs and my life, Luke. I am not sure I want to reinvest in another property. I have issues to sort out at the bank — to do with my voluntary redundancy — and I want to plan what I shall do next. This has made me think, but I am not sure it changes anything. I need space, my own space and time.'

She saw a flash of anger cross his eyes, or was it disappointment?

'I see, you know you could ask them to rescind your redundancy. You need to think about it on the flight. If holding down a day job and dealing with the cottages would be too much then I'll support you whilst you become the project manager, as it were. However, we need to put the new mortgage in place before you do anything rash. The world's changing, Jemma. The markets are going down and property is going to be cheap. Take this information and at least look them over. Just imagine one as our home, Jem. A cottage to decorate, that should be right up your street, once we've had them thoroughly damp-coursed and the fires sorted out. They have great potential. I'll phone you as soon as I can. Jemma, don't give up on us,' he said quietly into her ear, then kissed her gently on her lips at first, but then with an increasing urgency and passion.

She pulled herself gently away, aware

that emotions were being rekindled which had been the cause of her blurred vision where Luke was concerned. 'I'll think about them. OK? Come on, I have a plane to catch.' She was surprised that she felt herself bottle up with emotion. Wiping a tear away, she swallowed and went into the bathroom to freshen her face, wondering if she had misjudged him and the situation. Did he really love her? Was all this planning really for them both to share? Jemma prayed that by the time she touched down at Heathrow she would have the answers she needed. Part of her loved him, and always would, but she wanted what they already had, and he wanted what they could have in the future. The trouble was the future was always yet to come.

13

Airports always played havoc with Jemma's nervous system. On the outside she was as calm as a cookie, on the inside she harboured a complete hotchpotch of emotions: excitement, fear, apprehension, awe and wonderment that a heap of metal can actually take off by the use of sheer propulsion. There was much more to it than that, but as she had no interest in engines or physics, it remained one of the world's great mysteries. The red-tape made her nervous; the checks, scans, queues and passport control, more checks, all necessary in the troubled times of terrorism, all very daunting and unavoidable. This was neither her country, nor culture so here she was the foreigner and therefore possibly a perceived threat, the one to watch.

Luke had been the perfect considerate gentleman for once. So eager he had been to see she got on that flight, he had carried her bags, opened doors and sorted out where she needed to go — all very attentive; seeing to the luggage being checked onto the flight along with her, of course. Then with boarding pass in hand he had taken her to a coffee lounge, bought her a drink and a French pastry and held her hand in his when she had placed it on the table. Even this made her think back to her meal with Adam Li when he had done the same. The touch was very different. Luke's touch was firm and possessive. Adam's was exciting, her cheeks flushed slightly at the memory. She was a mature woman yet something about her brief encounter with this stranger made her feel young and alive again. The realisation that she hadn't felt this way for what seemed a long time shocked her.

'I've missed you, you know. I had hoped to spend five days here with you, retracing our first holiday in Penang.' He loosened his hold and started to play with her fingers gently as he spoke softly, as if remembering the time they were together. She wondered if he had sensed her emotions and misread them as tender memories of their time together. Then they had been completely absorbed with each other. 'If only the client had not taken so long to sign the contract we would have had that time. The bloody fool dallied; otherwise I'd have been out of Hanoi and here days before I was needed to head off to the Singapore office for the next stage of negotiations. I had it all planned for us to have a five day holiday between meetings. But you have enjoyed the trip, haven't you? I mean, you're glad you came out here, aren't you?'

He was trying so hard, she felt torn between the Luke that she was heartily fed up with and this revival of the Luke she had fallen in love with — the caring, attentive person who showed he valued her and her opinion. The trouble was in those few words he had encapsulated what was the problem with their relationship. He had planned it all out without stopping to consider that other people had their own agenda, including her. She would never have travelled so far dealing with jet lag on such a short break if she had known that he had not booked leave. He had merely planned that he would be able to control the events and people to give him the space he planned.

'Yes . . . I am, but it has given me time to think, Luke, and reflect on how much things have changed between us. You have such a demanding and well paid job, Luke, why do you need to risk it all on property at such a time when everyone is fearing global recession. We both had good jobs we could live perfectly happily.'

'Look, you know my job is important to me. You knew that before we moved in together. You should surely know you are too, but if we invest wisely now, in two or three years we could be spending lots of time together speculating.' He smiled and glanced up at the clock.

She felt just a little uneasy. Was this just an act which he was prepared to keep going until the hour passed and she would be through customs and out of his hair again? Then he would be off 'speculating' again whilst she was boarding the plane. She thought to test him. Why had he put his job first, before her? Jemma started to feel a little selfish, but he just wasn't the same as he used to be, or was it she who had changed and this was the real Luke? How could she know for sure?

'I think I had better go. I want to shop before boarding.'

'Great idea, buy yourself something nice to wear for our first date when I return. Put it on the card . . . make it sexy!' He winked at her as he picked up her rucksack that she always used as her flight bag. There was no hesitation, no squeeze of her hand, no look of sadness in his eyes, more relief that he would be free again to get on with his plans and, of course, his job. Her spirits lifted as he paused for a moment and looked thoughtfully down at her. Then she realised that it was only because he had noticed the side pocket of her rucksack, which was slightly ripped.

'Perhaps you should buy another of these. What happened to it?' Luke was very neat by nature. He did not like broken or damaged things; it let down the image he wished to project to the world.

Jemma had not realised until that morning that the bag had been damaged when the mugger had torn it off her. 'It must have ripped when the bag-snatcher grabbed it, or possibly when Adam knocked him off his bike.' She took hold of the bag's strap and slung it on her shoulder. 'It'll do for now.' She shrugged her shoulders as if dismissing it as unimportant, then realised, though, that those few words had been a real surprise to Luke. He almost looked shocked.

'What bag-snatcher, and who is Adam?' His smile had vanished. Jemma

138

saw a tinge of disbelief coupled with anger cross his face. She had not told him about her little 'adventure' and he was shaken by it, or was it the notion that he had known nothing about it. Jemma suspected the emotions he was now showing were the first genuine ones she had witnessed from him that morning.

They were walking to the check point beyond which he could not go. 'Not to worry, Luke. It happened so fast and I wasn't hurt.'

He took hold of her arm. With security and passport control police lining the customs points he had to act calmly. 'Tell me about it. If something happened to you, I should know. Why didn't you tell me if you have been in trouble? Were the police involved? Is that why you have been acting so irrationally?'

'Actually, Luke, you would have known all about it if you had contacted me earlier. It was outside that street restaurant that you insisted we meet at.

If it wasn't for the quick thinking of a total stranger, I would not have my bag at all. It happened very quickly, but it shook me up big time, never-the-less. So near the hotel too. In fact it may have been responsible for bringing me to my senses, I suppose.' She glanced at the gates. 'I must go. We'll talk in London in a week that is unless your people in Singapore have their own ideas of when they will sign your contract too. Whenever you turn up we will sort things out then.' She smiled at him politely, making no attempt to kiss him goodbye and set off on her own towards the customs' desks.

'Jemma . . . ' his voice stopped her for a moment.

Was he going to declare his love for her? Wish her a safe journey. Her hopes lifted a little.

'Who is Adam?'

His face was stern, as if she had kept a secret from him. Not just any secret but the name of a man. Perhaps, she thought, she had, with good reason.

'Adam is a 'have a go hero' who was in the right place at the right time. He saved me from being hurt and humiliated and retrieved the bag. No police were involved. I have to go, Luke, we'll speak in London.' She walked away not wanting to say more, but could feel him staring at her back as she went through the final checks before making her way to the shops and then on to the gate where her plane would be boarding.

Suddenly she did not feel nervous at all, but breathed deeply as she held her head high, enjoying a strange sensation — of being free.

14

The boarding hall seemed vast. Looking out of the window Jemma watched the planes dock, or taxi to the runway. It was a myriad of activity; passengers' belongings being taken from airport to plane and from planes to the eagerly waiting passengers in the arrivals halls. She could see their baggage trailers being loaded onto the aeroplane which would take her and her fellow passengers back safely — she hoped — to the UK. Soon she would be on her way and, as she saw another plane taxi and take off, she felt a childlike excitement growing inside her. This time she was going to make her own decisions and change the direction her previously planned out existence would take — planned out by Luke, not her.

There was a feeling of anticipation. People anxiously waited to see if they could be one of the first on to find their seat and claim their precious space. There was a tension as the first announcement calling people with young families to come forward to board the craft was made. Letters were then read out indicating blocks of rows of seats. Jemma felt no compunction to rush forward. She had her seat number and only had her rucksack to place on board so there would be no need to jostle to find a free overhead locker above her seat.

With an unusual calmness she wished the Malaysian airline air hostess 'Terimah kasih' which she hoped was the correct 'thank you' response to her greeting of 'Salamat datang'.

Jemma went down the aisle to her seat, hugged her battered rucksack to her, and fastened her seat belt securely around her waist. She put her hand in her jacket pocket and found the card Adam had left with her. She had not had the chance to look at it properly as Luke had arrived. She turned it over in her fingers and read the words that he'd written upon it:

'*Whenever, wherever, just phone. A.L.x.*'

It made her feel happy, wanted for herself. Like his brief kiss, it held promise of something in the future, restrained, as the time was not right. Everything had been rushed and compressed into a short meeting of minds and paths. Luke had even stolen some of her precious time with him, even if unwittingly because they had had to remove his drunken body from her door. She sat back, wondering at the change in her outlook on life and embracing this new personal optimism. In that moment of renewed spirits the plane taxied to the runway and she began her journey to a very different and exciting world.

★ ★ ★

Luke left the airport by taking a taxi and headed back towards the city and the hotel. The beauty of the flowers in the central reservation of the motorways was lost on him as was the hard work of the Indian gardeners who tended them in the humid heat. All he could think was, what was going on in that woman's head. Whatever it was, it was a mystery that troubled him. She hadn't fallen for the ring or the proposal as he had expected she would do, yet he had evaded getting hitched for nearly six months previously when he knew that was what she wanted. Each time she had subtly mentioned anything to do with rings, engagements or marriage he had pointed out that they had it all to look forward to. Jemma was being reserved with him, which was so unlike her. Why on earth hadn't she told him about the bag snatcher? She didn't appear to be physically harmed, which was a blessing, but something had changed within her. Why? Surely she hadn't blamed him for it. He stared at the row of flowers and shrubs which decorated the central aisle of the multi-lane carriage-way, not giving a thought to them but wondering if he arranged for a large bouquet of roses to greet her when she arrived in the UK, would that turn her back to being his Jemma? It might; he needed to think on it.

The driver approached the line of toll booths and swiped his card as they went onto another part of the roadway system which engulfed the growing city of Kuala Lumpur. With the air-conditioning on in the taxi it was cool, which helped to keep Luke's head and thoughts clear, unlike the stifling overbearing heat outside. As oil-palms drifted into the distance, they entered the city. Traffic queues made him feel anxious and frustrated. It was worse than London, this was a complete waste of his time. He should have taken a limousine and used his laptop but Jemma had played with his mind and he wasn't thinking straight. The hang-over had lifted but he was not himself. He wanted to go onto the internet in the comfort of his hotel suite, using his own trusted laptop and make sure that the funds were there in their account to use. He was going to secure the offer on the cottages before Jemma touched down. Then when she saw sense, the opportunity would not be lost. Jemma would come round, so they might have a few sulks if she found out he had pre-empted her decision, but he could ride the storm. She trusted his judgement, always had done, and not questioned him before, so why should she now? Her indecision must just be a reaction to the bag incident. That was it, post shock, it would explain everything. He laughed. At least it wasn't hormones. Perhaps she was trying to punish him for not being there and having to rely on this 'Adam' character. Who was he? Why hadn't she said anything about him? They could have taken the guy for a meal as a thank you.

When the taxi pulled up outside the hotel he pushed the ringgit at the driver and practically stormed off into the hotel. The doorman and the driver exchanged unheard comments in a language he wouldn't have understood anyway.

Luke put his hand in his pocket to retrieve his key card. Within moments he was in his room. He looked around, then something else connected in his brain: how had she known that he had been drinking Jack Daniels the previous evening? His head was in a strange blur over the previous evening's activities other than knowing he had been to her room. However, he was certain she was not there when he rang her door bell, because he had the ring in his hand still, so his task was incomplete. So how did he return to his room? He shook his head as he booted up the laptop. It was obvious, he must have walked, staggered back. Perhaps she had seen him in the restaurant. He dismissed that as highly unlikely because he would have seen her arrive. No, that was nonsense, she couldn't have or she would have joined him. It was then he remembered the interior designer guy who had been at her door when he had collected her that morning. What had she said the guy's name was — Adam L . . . someone?

Had she lied to him? Had he been saying his goodbyes? If so then from when? Or had he just left her room? Then he remembered walking past him in the restaurant. Luke couldn't remember if the guy was on his own, but he had been in the place, sitting in one of the other booths. An uneasy feeling gnawed at his stomach. No . . . Surely she wouldn't have . . . Dined in there knowing that he too was there waiting for her. What not with a stranger . . . Not with a . . . No! She'd only been in KL for five days, for goodness sake, and she knew he was trying to come to her, or should have. He couldn't bear the thoughts that were going through his head, a head which ached and hurt as his hangover seemed to be returning.

Luke logged onto his bank's home page. Well, it was the one Jemma worked at, or had done, the stupid girl, damn good job too, and they had a joint account for ease of access. He quickly filled in all the passwords and followed the security laden path which led to the account detail and ultimately to the balance.

He stared at the screen in disbelief. Yes, money had been transferred and was available for use, but only half of what he had expected was there. He pressed the button to reveal the account summary. Surely enough the total balance — the sale's profit — had been transferred into the account but, within a day of it clearing, the money had been split. Half had been moved into another account. Why would they do that? Jemma! What the hell was she trying to do to him? If she had planned to use this as leverage to get him to propose then it had all been unnecessary, but then that could not be right, for she had rejected his offer. Now he could not afford to put the option on the cottages through unless he cleared his own equity, taking all the risk himself, with no preferential rates to work with. What had happened to loyalty and trust? He'd shared his dream with this woman and she was going to cut and run from him . . . Why would she change so quickly?

He stood up, stretched and stared out of the window over the city. He saw a Chinese business man stepping out of a limousine and thought about the 'have a go hero'. This Adam guy must have worked quickly on her. He was forming a clear picture in his mind: one of a damsel in distress, how this guy steps from the crowd and wrestles a mugger to the ground, coming to her aid. He wondered if this guy worked with the so-called mugger to con stupid women. She is already vulnerable and unhappy, sitting on her own in a restaurant surrounded by strangers, her lover has not been there when she needed him. She thanks him, treats him to a meal and then money is mentioned and the cad moves in. Sometimes, he thought, she could be as gullible as a child. He knew it, but had this Adam chap sensed it too? He would phone her as soon as she touched down in England. No one did this to him!

He put his hand in his pocket and pulled out the small red box, the diamond ring still nestled within it. Well, Jemma Ward, if that's the way you want to play it, you're on your own, or will be once Adam has what he's after.

He flicked up his address book on the screen and looked up Trisha's contact details. No one would stop him achieving his goal. If one woman was too short-sighted to see what he could offer her, then there was another fish in the pond of his life who had better vision.

He dialled her number, the phone rang, stopped, and a message sounded in his ear, 'Hi, sorry I can't answer right now, but be a love and leave me a message after the beeps. Thanks!'

He sighed, she lacked style, but she was reliable or predictable, more so than Jemma had turned out to be. 'Hi, Trisha, it's Luke here. Hey, have I got something for you? E-mail me and we'll talk. I'll be back in Heathrow next Saturday around half two. Could you be a love and meet me there? I've got something special just for you. Love you, babe.'

He ended the call, smiled, and said out loud, 'Now back to business, and on to Singapore.'

★   ★   ★

Adam had taken a taxi back to the flat that he had in Chiswick. He had redesigned the interior and had been prepared to share it with Ling as they built their relationship and shared the space in harmony. He entered with just a little touch of apprehension, hoping that she would not still be there, wanting to avoid yet another futile confrontation. He was so relieved to see that Ling's wardrobe was empty. He had expected her to have left something for him to find — a threat, a Chinese cleaver or some such item of her affection, but to his surprise all there was an empty wardrobe.

From this open-space living room, he ran up the stairs to his roof space. Here he had his lovely planted garden. Miss Cholmondeley had promised to keep them watered if necessary while he was away. He had created an extended living space on the roof. It was another experiment which had worked. He had taken vast amounts of photos of it before going on holiday as he had plans to expand his business to incorporate open air living spaces too. Possibly even considered designing and writing a 'How to' book. He liked to keep new ideas bubbling and as the cliche said, doors open. He mused at the pun as he flipped open the roof door. It was then he understood what heartbreak truly was. Not one single pot or planter had been left whole. Not one plant still bloomed or survived. It looked as if weed killer had been poured on every flower bed, every plant, and every trellis fruit. Nothing remained neat, beautiful and complete. He swallowed back raw emotion as he saw one of his business cards had been ripped in two and each half nailed to the decking where once they had sat and laughed together. He would never love this space again. It had been hideously destroyed by the vengeful hand of hate. He would have to move. It was as if his dreams had been violated, but through the overwhelming numbness that threatened to consume him he knew one thing had not been destroyed — his idea, his dream, his ideals. He had never meant to hurt Ling, they would never have been happy together, but this sabotage against something he had poured hours of care into was bordering on evil.

Stunned, he returned to the open space below. Where fabric, wood and natural light blended and balanced. He would not tell his colleagues of his personal problems as that would make him vulnerable, and his business at least would be strong. Ling would have already blackened his name amongst their friends, no doubt. Now he would learn who was a true friend and who was not. He remembered Jemma's accurate description of him, when she said he had been running away. It made him wince, not a very noble thought, but accurate. Ling's temper had been an undisclosed secret which he had been stunned by once she had let it loose in front of him. The odd childlike tantrum had surfaced early in their relationship. She had been a single spoilt child, used to having her every wish supplied by her rich and powerful father. He had accepted that and hoped that it would calm and change once she stepped away from the parental influence and grew up in her own right, but he had not realised that she had no intention of doing that, she had wanted him to step under her father's influence too.

He had loved this place. It was light, airy and looked out over a busy tree-lined street. The sunlight beamed in falling across the parquet floor, giving a feeling of timelessness and peace until Ling had decided she had the right to start changing things.

He looked to the stairs that led out into the other cherished living space one he had created — the roof with its wealth of colour, mingled with a moderate supply of grow-your-own food planters, discreetly arranged to be a decorative feature, yet with a very practical function. All packed neatly together, it was a project he had put a lot of effort into it, deliberately so, as he had plans on extending his business into outside living spaces. He wanted to have his options open so that he could buck the trend or go with a new one if the recession hit.

What an excellent opportunity to explore concepts of growing your own foods in small areas at low cost and enjoying the experience and surroundings as you did so. Opportunity and flexibility were his best friends.

This vicious act was done out of

vengeful hatred. He thought for a moment about calling the police — this was vandalism at its worst. Then he thought of his business card, torn in two on the decking, the dragon side face down and the phoenix part staring up at him; a stoic message which had saddened him even more if that was possible. Once a place of romance and joy, it had become a place of confrontation and destruction. No, he would not report it. She had acted out of hurt, he now knew how it felt. But it only served to convince him that his decision to split from her was for the best. He would clear the mess with his own hands, change the locks on the doors and leave this part of his life behind him. Now was a time for him to move on.

15

Two weeks after returning to London, Jemma had moved into the back bedroom of a friend's house in a leafy suburb of Romford. It was not the perfect arrangement, but for a moderate rent it had provided her with a bolt hole where she could regroup and plan what to do next with her life. She was seriously considering following her dream and returning to college. She was gathering information about courses and working out the logistics.

When she first stepped into Heathrow she had been in a state, bordering on shock, when Luke had given her a welcome home present she never could have imagined. He had sent her a text. It simply stated, 'You have taken your half of MY profits — keep it. We're through. I'm shocked and disgusted. You used me.' She had just come through the 'nothing to declare channel' when she had switched on the phone to receive the insulting and hate filled message.

It had been such a blow to her self esteem because she had felt so positive through the long flight back home. She had even studied the information he had given her and was trying to view the deal objectively. At first she had been filled with hurt; she was going to try and explain what had happened and why she had transferred her half of the funds, to put a temporary brake on things. It was hers after all, by right, and not 'his' funds. Would he have gone ahead without her agreement if he had been able to transfer the whole amount? On the flight she had considered his offer of engagement and of the practicalities of renovating and living in the two cottages, but the funds had already been split. They were in need of a total overhaul. He would need his salary to oversee the renovation and there was a recession coming — what if he lost his job? Would he fly off around the world, chasing contracts whilst she made tea for the roofers, plumbers, plasterers or whoever they needed to complete the project. She had felt quite depressed at the thought, but then the prospect of meeting up with Adam again and asking his opinion had lifted her spirits until she had read the text.

When she had phoned the bank; it had been a decision made on the spur of the moment after they had disagreed and on the back of a verbal assault. It was out of her character, but then perhaps that was good, she had become like the welcome mat at home — walked on.

It had been a very wet day and the unexpected message had dampened her spirits further. So, whilst still jetlagged she had gone to her friend's house, without explaining why she and Luke were through, but she was temporarily without a home of her own.

All her calls sent to Luke's number since it had all fallen apart ended in

recorded messages, his phone perma-
nently on call divert. He was not going
to speak to her ever again, that was
certain, so she had drawn a line under
their relationship and started planning
her own path forward.

★ ★ ★

Luke arrived at Heathrow to Trisha's
welcome arms. They were what he
needed after Jemma's slight. She
listened as he told her how Jemma had
run off with half of his money and
taught him a valued lesson about
shallow women. He should never have
left his lovely, beautiful, Trish. He had
promised never to be such a fool again
and she had embraced him, and taken
his words to her very big heart and
bosom.

Trisha had a place in Romford; quite
a spacious one, near enough the busy
town centre for him to commute into
the city daily. He would be flying out
again within the month so it was a

home from home for him to plan from in between times. Two weeks had gone by and he had his things established there. He ignored Jemma's calls, she had missed her chance. The deposit on the cottages was down, he had paid it, but Trisha was moving out of her home, renting it out, whilst overseeing and helping to fund the renovation in the cottages. Convincing her to go along with him had been more straightforward than he had imagined. Life was starting to taste sweet again at the moment.

He turned the key in the lock and walked into the hall way. There she was, smiling and curvaceous. 'Hi, lover.' She gave him a hug and a welcome home kiss.

'I've got the contracts with me to sign. Do you fancy going out for a celebratory meal . . . partner? Then we can sign up and make arrangements for the remortgage to go through. You have been to the bank, haven't you?' Luke swept an arm around her waist and gave her a passionate kiss.

'Yes, I phoned them. Sounds like a great idea to me. I'll go and shower and change.' She picked up a glass of red wine and sipped it. 'Then we can talk about the wedding. I've booked a very simple civil service, and then we'll discuss where we book the meal for the families and friends.'

He laughed nervously. 'Plenty of time for that,' he said as he patted her behind. 'First things first. You already booked the date?'

'Yes, that's right, Luke. You told me that we would be married once before and look what happened. You met the girl wonder.' She smiled sweetly at him. 'I really don't want that to happen again, lover.' She was staring at Luke in a very direct manner.

'Trish, I explained about that and I'm very sorry. She bewitched me. It won't happen again, I told you I should never have fallen for her smooth talk, the devious minx.' He tried to look humbly at her, sorry — pathetic even. 'I have a trip coming up at work. I told you last week, so if it clashes then you'll have to rebook it for after I get back.' He winked at her.

'No, it won't clash. This time we go to the licence office. This weekend we marry with no frills. This Saturday, Luke, at 10.00 a.m. There is no reason in the world that will stop you being there, is there? I'll sort out a party for the family after your trip. But, Luke, I do love this ring.' She held up her finger with the solitary diamond set in a golden claw, which she wore with pride. 'I want the gold band to go with it before I re-mortgage my home. I'll not wait this time. You want me to be your partner in this property deal then we become a partnership for real — or no deal!'

She was standing on the stairs, hand defiantly placed upon her hip.

He looked at her, almost with respect. Not such a pushover after all. 'Okay! I keep my word, trust me this time. Make your arrangements but keep them simple. We need the money for the properties and our futures, Trish.' He blew her a kiss, resolved to his fate, then went into the living room and poured himself a Jack Daniels, muttering one word under his breath, 'Women!'

★   ★   ★

Adam had rented a flat near Canary Wharf, it had a balcony that looked out over the waterfront. He liked it here; it reminded him a little of Singapore in the way it was modern and cleaner than the old part of the city. He had picked up the reins of his business, removed all matter of the destruction of his roof eco-garden and with it had swept all the bitterness of Ling into the black bin bag in the process.

She had calmed down, apologised and offered to pay for the damage. She thought that would put everything right with them, all would be forgiven and put down to her volatile character. No doubt her father would give her the money without question, but Adam had taught her that money cannot buy everything in life you want. He and his business were not for sale. He had not heard from her again.

Instead, he rented this flat and was in the process of scouting the Docklands area for a new one. Then he had come across the piece of paper Jemma had placed in his hand, on which she had written a mobile phone number. He had nearly phoned three times previously but had put it off each time.

He was sitting outside a warehouse museum, his back to the old building, whilst looking at the new office, shops and flats opposite, and this time he didn't replace the paper in his wallet. His life was missing something, or someone, and try as he might he could not put his new friend out of his head.

She had most likely moved on in hers. He knew a woman like her was rare and, although he wished her well, he also wanted to be a part of her life.

He should also move on but, unless he made that call, he would always wonder if destiny had played a part in his life and if he had turned his back upon it.

He dialled the number and waited as her phone rang.

16

Jemma took the train to Liverpool Street station. She wanted to go to a couple of the major book stores and lose herself in the art and design section. Jemma found the books but all she could think about was a man called Adam Li. She became distracted and instead read everything about the Gold Coast and Sydney. She would plan her route, pick her time and just go. After that task was achieved she would drop by the outdoor clothing shops and buy a replacement lightweight rucksack to take on her next journey. If she was truthful, her life had lost its momentum: that of a regular work pattern and the need to consider a demanding partner, following a path which she hadn't wanted to embark upon. Freedom was liberating and daunting at the same time. Would she cope in a college situation? She wanted to do so much in her life. Her heart wanted to visit Australia, her head told her to start applying for a course in the area of interest she would be happy in. That was to do with interior furnishings, as she loved fabrics and wanted to design them herself, but where to begin? She didn't want to sell cushions in a department store, but she wanted to use her Art A level and return to college to learn the trade — like Adam had. There he was again.

That name constantly fluttered through her brain. Jemma even carried his card, promising herself that she would phone soon. She was halfway through a latte, with her mind engrossed in a book on New South Wales when, embarrassingly, her phone rang. She answered it quickly to shut it up, noting it was an unknown number.

'Hi,' she said.

'Jemma?' a voice replied.

'Yes, who's that?' The voice was slightly familiar — she hoped — she thought — she recognised it! Jemma put the book down on the coffee table and sat forward in the chair.

'Adam . . . Adam Li here. I wondered how you were getting on. You remember me, from KL. You're not still in Oz are you?'

'No . . . I mean, of course I remember you, but I'm not in Australia, I'm in London actually.'

'Great, so am I. Do you fancy having lunch and catching up? Are you free today?'

'Yes . . . sounds good to me. Do you mean, like, now?' She looked down at her old jeans — well they were at least clean.

'Yes, listen, I'm near Canary Wharf — where are you?'

He sounded keen; eager, even. Her heart quickened. This was silly, she was feeling like a teenager again. 'Near Shaftesbury Avenue,' she said quickly.

'Jemma, how about Dim Sum? You loved the pao in the hotel I know a great place in Gerrard Street. I can meet you in, say, an hour. Hang out in the crypt café of St Martins in the Field and I'll meet you there . . . My treat!'

'If I remember correctly it was yours last time we ate, it is mine this time.' Jemma laughed.

'Next time, it can be yours, okay?'

'Okay,' she agreed.

'See you in an hour.' He sounded so happy. He rang off.

Jemma looked at her phone. What had she done? Arranged a date for an hour's time, he had thought of a safe place for her to hang out whilst she waited for him. She would have to go just as she was: smart-casual. Jemma left the latte and the book and made for the street. She knew she would be early but she didn't care. Then she realised what he had said and what she had so readily agreed to — the next date would be her treat. There would be another date. She smiled so wide and, with a bounce to her step she made her way beyond Leicester Square, past Trafalgar Square to the famous church of St Martins, taking the lift to the crypt of the mighty building.

★ ★ ★

When she saw Adam appearing in the lift a while later, Jemma felt an inner warmth as he smiled when he saw her, and she recognised the mutual light show in his face.

'You look great,' he said casually, as he walked over to her.

'Likewise,' she replied without hesitation, as he did. Smart-casual yet stylish.

He placed an arm loosely around her waist and led her back out onto the street. He took hold of her hand, gave her a kiss on the cheek and led the way back towards China Town.

The streets were teeming with people so they didn't really have time to talk to one another until they were seated in the vast restaurant. Jemma watched as he spoke in Mandarin and ordered some of the dishes that she had told him she liked in the hotel in Kuala

Lumpur, so far away in miles and what seemed like another time completely. Here he was and he remembered her favourites. Adam was the one person she had thought about more and more. More than she had Luke.

'How are you?' He looked at her, but shifted position. 'I've been meaning to phone ... ' The small plates were brought to the table as the girl served pao from the steam trolley. The bamboo baskets were arranged on the table in front of them.

'So have I. Luke and I split, no going back now. He wouldn't even talk to me once he found out I had my share of the profit moved to my own account. Thought I'd cut and run but it wasn't like that. I just wanted time to think before he committed the funds to yet another scheme.'

'Great!' He instantly looked guiltily at her.

'Yes, it is. We weren't right together, Adam. I never felt quite like this about a new friendship ... I ... '

174

Another trolley arrived and she did not finish the statement but they both stared into each other's eyes and, as he waved the trolley on, there seemed no reason to finish it.

17

From the restaurant they walked around Trafalgar Square, making their way down Horse Guards to the Embankment. As afternoon turned into evening it was as if neither wanted to walk away from the other. Jemma looked at the river as they lazily leaned against the wall. 'I had better make my way back to Romford.'

'Why?' he asked, and reached an arm out to her. She curled into him as if it was the most natural place on earth to be.

'Because that is where I am living at the moment.'

'You have bought somewhere?' he asked, as he kissed her forehead.

'No, staying with a friend. I'm looking for something more permanent.' She looked up at him. 'Adam, we hardly know each other.' She saw him grin.

'I know, it doesn't make sense, does it? We're moving too fast, but since we left KL I haven't passed a day when your face has not been in my head. I can't get on with my plans until I solve the puzzle — which is you.'

'I've been the same. I need to find a course or a job. I'm technically on the rebound, so how do I know what I feel is real, Adam?' They kissed, which only helped to confuse Jemma more because what she was feeling was definitely real and right.

When she finally tilted her head back and looked at him, he reminded her of the cat who had found the cream, his eyes so full of fun, his face so full of hope and his embrace so welcoming, protective and warm.

'I have a possible solution, I think.' He took her by the hand and led her to a seat.

'Adam, I don't think that we can sort things out this quickly,' she began to say, but then he placed a finger to her lips.

'Shh, my little phoenix, you are thinking too much. It is time you rose from the ashes of uncertainty and I woke up the dragon once more.'

She could not speak. He looked totally embarrassed as they fell back aginst the bench laughing at themselves. 'You are so funny,' she said.

'So are you,' he answered before their lips were too busy kissing once more to waste time speaking.

★ ★ ★

Trisha phoned her mother. 'Yes, Mum, it's all set. 10 a.m. on Saturday morning. You and Dad okay to be there? Great!'

She sipped her glass of wine. 'No, Mum, I'm not drinking, why do you think I would? No, not in my condition.' She walked over to the sink and poured the wine away. 'Yep, that's right, I've changed, I'm going to be a great wife and a fantastic mother just like you. Being pregnant is making me a more responsible person — honest.' She laughed. 'Look, I'll have to go, Luke is due anytime. No, I haven't told him yet, it will be a surprise — my wedding present to him. After all, he's definitely showing nesting leanings, buying a cottage and all. He'll be thrilled. We'll celebrate together on Saturday. Bye, don't be late. Love you!'

Adam took Jemma to Canary Wharf and showed her the apartment he had just placed a deposit on.

'Well, what do you think?' he asked her looking at her with apprehension. The view over the river was spectacular. The open living space was light and airy and the three bedrooms off it were also well presented.

'I love it, Adam, but . . . '

'What?'

'I . . . I am a little nervous of mixing business with pleasure . . . ' She was lost for words again. How could she explain to this man that she didn't know what he was asking her, and why she was really there?

'Jemma, rent a room here. No obligation to do anything else on a personal basis. No pressure. We take it slow. You have your life I have mine. Flat mates! See how we get along sharing a living space. Work with me, be an apprentice to my company. You go to college, follow your dream and work for the experience for 'Living Spaces'. That way, we find out exactly if we can work together and if it is right for us to do so. In our own time we decide if we want to make any other kind of commit-ments — if we do, then let it be so. If not, then move on, you're free to fly.'

Jemma looked out at the river running its course. She glanced at the open blue sky and then turned back to face Adam. Instantly she felt warm as if her own personal inner sun was shining.

'Yes . . . Adam, I think I will. I can't make promises about anything but I will work hard and I like a clean and happy home.'

His impish smile appeared again.

'Great, I shall have to make sure that you are kept happy then.' He swung her off her feet. 'No pressure,' he repeated.

'None,' she said, as she wrapped her arms around his neck, loving the feelings that flowed through her whole body. Her future had just been revealed to her, she had a friend, she had a vision and they had a future. Destiny had played its part. 'No pressure,' she repeated, as her head fell against his chest and he swung her around. She laughed out loud, knowing absolutely none would be needed.

THE END

A KISS AND A PROMISE

Moyra Tarling

Just as Autumn Daniels is getting her life back together after her husband's death, Matt Kingston returns. He'd left her five years ago with a kiss and a promise he never kept. Then, pregnant and alone, she'd turned to his brother — however, his proposal of marriage was just an elaborate scheme of vengeance. But now, as Matt melts the ice around her heart, is it Autumn he wants — or his daughter? This time, is his promise of love forever?

TOMORROW'S PROMISE

Gillian Villiers

Lara is determined never to risk falling in love, but when she takes up a new teaching post, finds it isn't quite so simple. She shares a house with fellow teacher Mick, whose laid-back manner hides a warm heart that threatens to melt even Lara's cool exterior. Trying to distract herself with a spot of property development only seems to involve her in endless problems, which Mick is more than happy to help resolve. But should she let him?

FOLLOW YOUR HEART

Margaret Mounsdon

Marie Stanford's life is turned upside down when she is asked to house sit for her mysterious Aunt Angela, who has purchased a converted barn property in the Cotswolds. Nothing is as it seems . . . Who is the mysterious Jed Soames and why is he so interested in Maynard's? And can she trust Pierre Dubois, Aunt Angela's stepson? Until Marie can find the answers to these questions she dare not let herself follow her heart.